ENEMY HEIR

CARRIE ANN RYAN
NANA MALONE

ENEMY HEIR

A TATTERED ROYALS NOVEL

By
Carrie Ann Ryan & Nana Malone

ENEMY HEIR
A Tattered Royals Novel
By: Carrie Ann Ryan & Nana Malone
© 2021 Carrie Ann Ryan & Nana Malone
eBook ISBN: 978-1-950443-46-8
Paperback ISBN: 978-1-950443-47-5

Cover Art by Sweet N Spicy Designs
Photograph by Wander Photography

ENEMY HEIR

Chapter 1
SPARROW

A royal pain in my...

"IN ORDER OF BADASSERY, the library fight, from *John Wick*; *The Bourne Identity* pen fight; the living room fight from *Mr. and Mrs. Smith*; and as my John Wick closer, the *John Wick* club fight."

Wilder Waterford rolled his eyes. "That's your final answer? You can't have two John Wicks in there."

I sighed and rolled my eyes. "Okay, fine then. Replace one with *The Matrix*."

He snorted. "We said in the last fifteen years. Neo doesn't count."

I scoffed. "Does too. Honorable mention."

Wilder's shoulders shook as he laughed. "You have to follow the rules."

"We said best hand-to-hand-combat scene in a movie. Those are the best ones. And before you tell me I can't use *Mr. and Mrs. Smith*, I'm going to say fight me, because not only did it have great hand-to-hand, it was also funny and sexy."

He threw up his hands. "I didn't know those were the criteria."

I shrugged. "Let's just call it a woman's prerogative."

"Sparrow, I swear to God. I'll give you *The Matrix*. I'll give you *John Wick*. But *Mr. and Mrs. Smith*?"

"Fight me."

There was something about the way he laughed, a flirty undertone. "Hey, there's a fantastic gym here anytime you want to spar."

I sized him up. "Well, you are a prince, so I'm pretty sure it's against the law to kick your ass."

His chuckle was low and mellow, pleasant sounding. And it did absolutely nothing for me. Wilder was exceptionally handsome. Sadly, he gave me brother vibes. Not that I had time for a personal life. I was too busy with work. And, if I was honest, I wasn't even in that frame of mind.

And he's not the brother you want.

I squashed the thought of Breck Waterford the moment it popped into my head. I *loathed* him. He was the literal worst. If there were something worse than loathing, that *might* encompass the breadth of my feelings for the prince.

Also, you think he's fuckable.

Shit. That too.

"Well, I mean, I know you've been injured recently, so I wouldn't want to hurt you," Wilder teased.

I lifted a brow. "Anytime, Your Highness. Anytime."

He grinned, knowing it would get my hackles up. "All right, I hear you. By the way, I've got a clearance for the rest of your team should they get into trouble—a diplomatic pass. Is there anything else you need?"

"You mean besides you finally admitting that my list of movies is far superior to yours? No, I'm good." I glanced toward the window and frowned. The clear blue sky had given way to a pale purple hue. "What time is it?"

He inclined his head toward the clock behind me. "Just past seven."

Damn. I needed to get out of there. Dinner was first on the agenda. I hadn't eaten a bite since breakfast. "Geez. I was supposed to make a phone call. I'd better get home. Thank you for this meeting, though. I'll be back to go over the other security protocols."

"My doors are always open for you."

"Thanks for making this easy on me, Wild. With Kannon and London on vacation, you've really helped me see to it that things go smoothly as we get ready for the company's official European opening. It's easier with your help."

"Anytime. Besides, we're practically family now," he said with a shrug.

I wrinkled my nose. "Wait, does this mean I inherit Breck too?"

He laughed at that. "Yes, sadly. The whole family comes with Breck *and* Roman."

I wrinkled my nose even more at that. "Fine, we can keep Roman. He's okay, but can we put Breck up for adoption?"

Wilder snorted. "Roman's very taken with you."

"Ah, he's just a big grizzly bear. I know how to handle guys like that. I mean, he's a king, so that's a whole other level, but at the core of it he loves his family, loves his people. He just likes to roar, and you have to show that you're not going to hide from the roar. Then you can be friends."

"I wonder how he would take it if he knew you summed him up so easily."

I shrugged. "He's not an easy read, mind you. But my whole job is to read people."

"That's hardly your *whole* job."

"Maybe not my whole job, but there's a lot of that." I

pushed out of my chair, and my stomach growled and rumbled.

"Oh, damn. I should have fed you. Sorry. We got to work, and I lost track of time. Do you want to stay for dinner?"

I considered his offer. I had a standing call date with my friend Onyx that night. I could call her later, but there were some things that I needed to do in the office first, anyway, and eat. "No, that's okay. I'll go home. I'll have a glass of wine, throw on some yoga pants and really let my hair loose, and then I'm going to go over the schematics for the new building."

He clutched a hand to his heart. "Oh God, you're speaking my language with all that schematics talk."

"I know. Clearly, I have no life. I just want everything perfect by the time Kannon gets back. You know, so he'll see his faith in me isn't misplaced."

Wilder's light blue gaze met mine. "He'll know that. I promise. I can see it. You're more than capable enough. You could be running this company."

"No. Kannon's the leader. But while he's gone, I will hold down the fort."

"You do that. Thank you for the company as always. You know, terrible movie choices notwithstanding."

I rolled my eyes. "I know you're a prince, and you're

used to getting your way. But sooner or later, you will just realize that I'm right. We need a tie-breaker."

He crossed his arms then. "Who would I approve of as a tie-breaker?"

We met each other's gazes and laughed and nodded our heads as we both muttered, "Kannon."

"Let's regroup at the end of the week. And if you need anything else before then, just text me."

I gathered my folders and slid them into my shoulder bag. "I will. Thanks, Wild."

"Later, Sparrow. And just in case you were wondering, I'm glad you're here. At least there's someone else I can finally chat with. Breck hardly has any interest in security, and Roman only cares about the end result. So you're a breath of fresh air."

"I aim to please."

"Do you need a map out of here?"

I narrowed my gaze at him. "Too soon," I muttered while laughing. My first time in the palace, I'd gotten turned around. I was always getting lost, never seeming to find the right way back to where I was trying to go. Which was how I'd run into his brother Breck, shagging two women, in what I thought was my bedroom.

I'd turned around and found a different path toward my room. It turned out they were in a spare guest room and not the one that had been assigned to me. The passcodes were always the same in that sector of the palace for the guest quarters. I'd been less than thrilled and, I had to admit, a little awed by his flexibility, when I found Breck screwing two women on what I thought was *my* bed. Except, it hadn't been *my* bed. So that had been awkward to say the least.

The whole thing was made more awkward because I hadn't been able to stop staring at him. He was no soft playboy. Instead he was ripped with muscles for days. He sure as shit didn't get that kind of physique from fencing alone. And from where I'd been standing, he appeared to be very talented with his mouth and hands.

I cleared my throat to help shake the image of Breck and his magic tongue. "Very funny. And nope, there's no need. I've got it now. I burned the map into my head."

He chuckled softly. "Okay, if you say so. Have Thomas or whoever is working security at the gate walk you to your car."

"Sure. Will do."

But I wouldn't. I appreciated the safety concerns, but it was just about a hundred meters to the car. I'd be fine. As much as I appreciated the whole 'you're family now' song and dance, I didn't love the overbearing-big-brother thing.

I took a left out of Wilder's office toward the North Tower. But before I could make it to the safety of the cobblestones and the gate, I saw the one person in the entire palace whom I'd hoped *not* to see, and he froze when he saw me. *Breck Waterford.*

Our gazes locked, and my belly did a flip flop. *Stop it. You don't even like him. Besides, he's no doubt drunk again.*

I faltered for a moment, making that mental calculation of whether or not I could avoid talking to him. But no. He was already walking toward me.

"Hello, Feisty."

I rolled my eyes and set my jaw. There was no avoiding him now that he'd seen me. "Your Highness." The words were ones of respect, but I couldn't keep the irritation out of my voice.

His grin was quick. "Ahh, there is that warm welcome I've come to expect from you. One of these days, you'll need to tell me why you don't like me. I mean, everybody likes me. Haven't you heard? I'm a prince."

"Oh, I've heard. I've seen, um, all your assets, such as they are. I'm just not particularly impressed."

Liar. I was *such* a liar. That eyeful I'd gotten when I walked in on him with the two supermodels proved his assets were just fine. Enormous actually. To the point of jaw dropping. It was no wonder he trotted out his... *assets* every chance he got. But I'd walk across hot coals before I ever said anything like that to him. His playboy exploits were legendary. I'd only just moved to Alden and, so far, every eligible female I'd run into had some Breck story.

And from the stories I'd heard, he had every right to be arrogant.

My skin flushed just thinking about him. Or maybe the heat was a result of his closeness. Even if I found him arrogant, irritating, and brash, he had sex appeal in spades. Unlike Wilder, there was not a single brother vibe in sight.

Nope. Breck Waterford had my number. But like hell was I telling him that.

"You keep on denying you feel that pull between us. Look, I get it. I'm sexy. You can't help yourself."

I scowled at him. "Seriously? You're disgusting."

He laughed. "Who are you kidding, Feisty? I can see it in your eyes. Pupils dilated. Lips parted. That honey skin all flushed."

"So, you're telling me that your whole life women have told you were appealing? I'm so sorry to disappoint you, Your Highness. But I won't be one of those women."

"Sure you will. You just haven't gotten there yet. Pretend you don't like me all you want. But I know the truth."

"Okay, Breck. If this whole act you put on works for you, keep it up. It just doesn't work for me. I loathe arrogant guys. You forget, I've seen your skills. Completely unimpressive. Hell, I've even seen bigger."

Again with the lies. I should be ashamed of myself, but my training had taught me, when in dire straits, use all the tools at your disposal. And so, until I made it to safety, I needed to treat his presence as hostile. I needed to use any tactic I could, period, to escape before I did something dumb like lean in and sniff him.

Why did he smell so damn good?

He clutched a hand over his heart. "Oh, Feisty. You wound me. Or at least you would if I didn't already know who you were working with. But you tell yourself whatever you need. I promise you that you're sniffing around the wrong brother."

I frowned as he brushed past me, the minor contact making my nipples peak. "What the hell is that supposed to mean?"

Breck rolled his eyes. "You don't think I see you and my little brother? Sure, he's the upstanding one. But he has his... tastes." He smirked at that. "Who knows? Maybe you're into it, which makes me incredibly sad it isn't me that you want."

"I beg your pardon, but you're the worst, Your Highness."

"Try harder to pretend, Feisty." His voice was a low hum as he muttered over his shoulder.

God, what was it about him that made my whole body vibrate? What I wanted to do was follow him and keep fighting. Yet, not five minutes ago, I'd been starving and needing to crash.

But one Breck sighting and I was ready for a fight. An all-out grudge match. He could do that to me, make me relinquish my carefully constructed control. Maybe that was why I didn't like him. I knew what was good for me. And staying the hell away from Breck Waterford was at the top of that list.

Chapter 2
SPARROW

What doesn't kill me...

I WASN'T sure how long I stood in the hallway staring after the prince.

Jesus Christ, Sparrow, get a hold of yourself. He's only a prince. It's not like you don't know another one. You even know a king now. Breck Waterford isn't unique.

This had to stop. I needed to figure out a way to get my shit under control when I was around him. Shaking off my run-in with him, I marched toward the courtyard. I now knew the little arrows on the giant statues in the courtyard pointed you in the right direction.

So I just had to follow the statue facing the north hallway, which I did, easily. Even after several months, the palace completely awed me. It was something akin to a Cinderella fantasy world. There were all these parapets and so much white stone. Inside, the floors were marble, the walls covered in priceless art, ceilings painted by the masters. It was gilded opulence everywhere you turned. I had expected the same thing in the guest rooms, but those had all been remodeled and refurbished—ultra modern with all the conveniences.

It must have been amazing for London to grow up here. I'd grown up between DC and Mauritius. My father was a diplomat, and my mother was a professor from Mauritius. There were many trips home, as my mother called it. And, if I was being honest, Mauritius felt more like home to me than DC ever had.

There was a frenzy to DC. People were always moving, never stopping. And there was something about Mauritius that was settling, calming in the blood. If I'd grown up somewhere like here, I was convinced I would have burned every hallway, every painting into my memory. I wondered if that was how London felt. I liked her a lot. And, as an added bonus, she made Kannon so happy. I couldn't have picked better for him myself.

At the gate, I waved at Thomas, who was on guard duty. "Have a good night, Thomas."

"Miss Bridges, would you like me to walk you to your car?"

I sighed. I should, but the idea making of idle small talk for the next hundred meters was too much. "It's right there, Thomas. I can see it from here."

Yes, there were some shadows along the way to the parking lot, but it was the *palace* parking lot. And there were a few other cars. Most of the staff hadn't yet gone home for the night. "Look, I know Wilder wants you to do that, but it's fine. You can watch me from here. You'll see me on the security cameras anyway."

"If you say so, ma'am." I thought he'd fight me, but he didn't. He was looking at something on his phone, so clearly he was already preoccupied. "Have a good night. I'll see you later."

"See you."

The gate buzzed, and out I went, pausing momentarily to inhale the warm summer air. I loved the summer season, the scents of flowers in the air, the warm breezes, it was perfect.

I was excited that Kannon had chosen me to join the team in Alden. I could have stayed in Los Angeles, and it would have been great. I could have run that office on my own. But I felt like there was more opportunity here. Besides, on this side of the world, I'd be closer to my best friend, Onyx, who lived in the UK. While I enjoyed LA, it was really more about the people than anything. I reached my car, unlocked it, went to the trunk and slid in the files that I carried with me, then opened the driver's side door.

Before I slid in, though, I heard a noise. It sounded like something scratching around on the other side of the car. Frowning, I peered around, but I couldn't see anything. I'd parked two spaces away from an entry of some sort, but it wasn't one of the lit corners. A shiver ran up my spine, and I suddenly regretted not having Thomas walk me to the car. But I merely scolded myself as I turned on the flashlight on my keychain. I walked around and spied the rustling silver wrapper of a bag of chips.

I went to pick it up, wondering who would dare litter in the royal parking lot. The voice behind me was a low menace from the shadows. "This is almost too easy."

I felt, rather than saw, the arm coming overhead. Not even thinking, I dropped my keys and lifted my hands up over my head and blocked the shot. I planted my feet and lowered my body weight, shifted my shoulder back, and used his own momentum to flip him.

It was a lot of weight, but the move was guaranteed to work. Always.

Male. Maybe six feet. Just under two hundred pounds.

He rolled out of my grip and got to his feet quickly, hands up.

I opened my mouth to scream because it was not the time to be a solo badass. But before I could make a sound, he jabbed quickly. Pain exploded on my cheek, and the scream was caught in my throat as I staggered backward. Then he was on me, his hands on the back of my neck like a modified clamp. He attempted to knee me in the stomach, but I blocked him as I caught the underside of his knee then flipped him onto his back. He yowled as he slammed hard onto the ground.

Wasting no time, I drew from all my training and jumped on him, panting. I punched him, delivered hit after hit. My legs locked around his waist, and using all the energy I could muster, I delivered straight punches, hammer fists and elbows, refusing to let up. Luckily, my training helped me remember to question him. "Who sent you?"

His lips started to move, and then I saw them lift into a sneer. "Fuck. You."

I tsked. "Oh, that's pleasant."

I lifted an elbow and dropped it right onto that tender spot on his shoulder joint. Quick, sharp, and he yowled again. I'd seen him telegraph his punches on that side and thought he must have some kind of injury.

I lifted his head up by the front of his hair. "Who sent you?"

I heard a sound behind me, and out of my periphery, I checked for a movement in the shadows, but there was nothing there. But in that one second of inattention, I gave my attacker the advantage. He lifted his hips, flipping me over onto my back until I landed on the hard pavement with a wince as the cold rock did a number on my muscles.

I put my hands up to block, anticipating a blow at any moment. When he didn't immediately attack, I rolled over and pushed myself to my feet, jumping up. I watched as he yanked open the doorway to our right, wheezing in pain, and stumbled through to the dark alley beyond. From my left, I saw Thomas heading our way. "Miss Bridges, are you okay?"

I waved down at my feet, exhaustion hitting me as the adrenaline receded. "I'm okay, but I needed you to call the palace guard. Someone just attacked me."

Thomas was on his walkie talkie before I even finished my request. And as I sank down onto the cold ground, no longer able to keep my body weight up, I scowled. Who the hell was that? And why the hell did he seem so familiar?

The last thing I was aware of before the darkness encroached on my vision was Wilder's voice. "Sparrow.

Jesus Christ, Sparrow. Thomas, why didn't you walk her to the goddamn car?"

The guard stammered, "She told me she didn't want me to."

There was more talking, but their voices went in and out, and I couldn't focus on them. One voice filtered in though, making me feel hot and prickly. "Jesus fucking Christ, what happened to her?"

"Breck, I need you to pull the security camera feed from the parking lot and the access doorway here. Scratch that, get me every view from the palace and the main road, got me?"

Breck said something else. And then, "God, is she hurt?"

There were fingers pressed to my wrist, and I struggled to hold on to consciousness. I opened my mouth to speak a strong, tired, "No. I'm fffnnn...."

I frowned. That didn't sound like it made sense. I tried again. "Ssslung, ssstand up."

I dragged my eyelids open, trying to look around me, and Wilder's handsome face was in my direct line of sight. But it was close. Too close. I swung my gaze around and caught Breck's gaze next. What was he doing here? I tried to push him away, but his hands were too strong.

"All right, help me lift her up."

Then there were many hands and much more talking and voices. I had a sense of being moved. I wasn't sure how long or what route we took, but I could only guess we were in the infirmary. When we stopped, I detected that antiseptic smell. And then I was laying on something soft and plush, and I could hear beeping, and people bustled around me, and there were sounds and smells of doctor things.

That was all I had total awareness of before I passed out.

WHEN I CAME TO, Wilder was there in the chair next to my bed. "Ah, there you are. You gave us all quite a scare."

I groaned. When I tried to lift my head, it throbbed. "Ugh, what happened?"

"I was hoping you could tell me that."

"Where am I?"

"You're in the palace infirmary. I had my personal doctor check you out. You had a bump on the head. No concussion though. You've sustained bruises and cuts but no real damage. You have some abrasions on your knuckles as well, likely from where you hit whoever attacked you."

I frowned. He sounded annoyed. Why was he annoyed?

I licked my lips. So dry. "Why are you mad at me?" I had a father. His name was Steven, not Wilder.

"I remember giving you distinct instructions to have Thomas walk you to your car."

I'd known this was coming. "Well, it was only a hundred meters."

"I gave you a direct order."

Oh hell no. "Is this the part where I remind you that I'm not one of your subjects?"

He expelled a long breath. "You just fought off an attacker, *on palace grounds*, lived to tell the tale, and judging by the abrasions on your knuckles, gave him some food for thought. So right now, I'm trying to be grateful. But I'm peeved, and we're going to talk about this whole not-listening-to-sound-caution thing when you feel better."

I groaned and tried to sit up again. "When can I go home?"

He sighed. "Other than some bruises, there's not much wrong with you. They'll keep you overnight for observation since you were in and out of consciousness, but they'll probably discharge you in the morning."

I wanted to argue, but he was right. I'd taken a risk for no good reason other than Breck had irritated me, and I'd been in no mood to talk to anyone. "Thanks, Wild. I appreciate it."

He blinked his eyes. "I know you don't take orders well, but you should have just listened."

"I know. I should have. And I didn't. My bad."

When he spoke again, his voice was gentler. "Are you okay?" His frown set grooves in his handsome face. Again, he had that big brother vibe to him. I was unaccustomed to scolding.

"I guess I'll be fine. You should see the other guy."

The corners of his lips ticked up in a small smirk. "I hope you gave him the ass-kicking he deserved."

"If I'd had more time, oh the damage I could have done."

"Something tells me you had plenty of time and inflicted plenty of damage. But next time do me a favor; listen when I tell you to have someone walk you to your bloody car."

"Next time I will listen. You don't have to tell me twice."

"Did you get a good look at him? Recognize him?"

I shook my head. "I have no idea why anyone would want to jump me. But I got the feeling he was waiting for me."

"Do you always park there when you come to the palace?"

CARRIE ANN RYAN & NANA MALONE

I shook my head. "No. I just took the open slot."

"We'll check the cameras. Breck's on it now."

I groaned. "Okay, but if you don't mind, I'll call Olly and see if he can have a look. Nikolai is here too. I'll have him look as well."

Wilder looked like he wanted to argue. "Look, I get it, you and Breck are like oil and water. Hell, I even understand why. My brother is a pain in the ass. And yes, he's always been like that. But I promise you, he's good at what he does."

"So is my team." I didn't trust Breck as far as I could throw him, but just the mention of his name had my skin prickling. Why did he do that to me? It was the last thing I wanted, the last thing I *needed*. And why was it that the one brother who was obviously emotionally unavailable, a giant pain in the ass, and the worst kind of choice was always the one I was interested in? Not the handsome, stable, kind one.

I didn't know why, but my body responded to the one who took playboy to a whole new meaning. "I appreciate it, Wild. Honestly, I do. And you didn't have to do this. I'm okay." But as the smile tried to take over, my cheek burned.

What was it about assholes? Did some asshole academy gather them at some unknown location and teach them all how to hit just right across the face? God, that stung. But I needed to show Wilder that I wasn't in any kind of pain. Otherwise, he'd keep it up with the nursemaid routine. "Honestly, I could probably go home tonight."

He lifted a brow. "You could. But I'd just insist that the only way that is going to happen is through me. And then, of course, well, you'd be forced to challenge me. And if you thought you could actually get through me, it would be a sight to behold."

I sized him up. Fully healthy, I might not win in the challenge, but I could land some really good hits. But not like this... "Why challenge you? I just think it's ridiculous. I really do feel fine."

Lies.

"Uh-huh, fine. You realize you've been unconscious for the last hour?"

"Jesus."

"Like the doctor said, it's likely you're fine, but they want to keep you for observation. I insist."

The way he'd said that word *insist* made it sound like it was a command. He pushed to his feet and then took my hand and squeezed it. "I'm making you promise. If you were a citizen of Alden, I could prosecute you for disobeying me."

I squeezed back and winced as his thumb accidentally rubbed one of my abraded knuckles. "Fine. Twist my arm, why don't you?"

"I'll do what I have to."

He released me and then turned to go. But when he reached the door, I called out. "Hey, Wild?"

He turned with a tight smile. "Yes, Sparrow?"

"Thank you. You didn't need to do all this, and I appreciate it."

He gave me a slight nod. "As I said, you're practically family now. So I'm taking this attack very, *very,* personally. We'll figure out who the hell came for you."

Chapter 3
BRECK

...makes her stronger.

"YOU NEED TO LEAVE HER BE."

I gritted my teeth and moved past my brother's immense shoulders to get to Sparrow's room.

Or at least I tried to. Wilder moved again, and I scowled at my younger brother.

"She's sleeping, Breck. She needs rest."

I snorted. "Like the Wicked Witch of the West could actually sleep? Knowing Feisty, she's probably plotting my demise."

Wild's light blue eyes narrowed. "I don't know what the hell is with the two of you, but she was hurt, on our grounds, under our watch. So we are going to figure out what the hell happened. To do that, you are going to put aside your cocksure attitude and get the job done."

I lifted a brow. "A little overprotective of our sweet Sparrow, aren't you?"

I didn't know why a kernel of jealousy slid through me. It wasn't as if I wanted her. Sure, she was hot as hell with her honey-toned skin, sinful curves that were all softness melded with strength and muscle, and long dark hair. But I didn't want her.

Besides, it was hard to crave somebody when they constantly sneered at you and derided you for being a playboy piece of shit. To be fair, I had done my best to keep up that reputation, but I didn't need Sparrow judging me for it. Enough people in my world judged me already.

"I'm going to need your help, Breck."

It was unusual for Wilder to ask me for anything. I was the family fuck-up, as it were. "Sure, whatever you need. I'm just going to go check on her, okay?" I asked, not even sure why I wanted to do so. Sparrow wanted nothing to do with me, and had made that fact plainly clear. But I'd gotten used to her little scowls. I wondered if that expression could be kissed off.

What?

Not by me of course. Because... no. But she'd prob-

26

ably be in a much better mood if someone shagged her properly.

I still remembered the time she had walked in on me, and I hadn't exactly been in the best position. I'd had my ass on display, my mouth on a very delectable pussy and my fingers in another pussy altogether. Not ideal, admittedly.

She'd stared at me, pretty full lips parted in shock, and I had smirked right back and kept going along with my business. It was easier to keep people at a distance by grinning and pretending nothing mattered.

Except it did matter.

I just wasn't a huge fan of the idea that Sparrow was so swift to judge.

"Be quick about it," Wilder muttered.

I blinked to bring myself back from my reverie. I narrowed my eyes at his tone. "Something going on between you two?"

Wilder had this way of wiping all hint of expression off his face. I recognized it as his protection wall. "I don't know why you would think that. Unlike you, I know how to be friends with a woman without wanting to get in her pants."

"Sometimes they aren't wearing pants. Sometimes you can ruck up their skirts and take them right there. As long as they're willing, able, and wanting, why not?"

"You truly are the arsehole everyone claims you to be sometimes, big brother."

I shrugged and shoved past Wilder into the infirmary. There was nobody else in the room; the nurse and the doctor had gone to their offices. We were lucky that we didn't have to use this place too often. Usually, it was for minor scrapes or issues, but more recently, it was being used for my baby sister's pregnancy. Now there was a single person in the lone bed with her sheets up to her neck and a scowl on her face as she slept.

I held back a snort. Well, at least the scowl was usual for her. She didn't look any different.

Liar.

Her skin looked soft, and yet I saw the bruises there, saw the pain she must have been in when she'd been attacked.

Who the hell had come at her? I had heard she fought back and took down the attacker, and I would've liked to see that.

Whatever my problems were with Sparrow, I loved the way that she moved. She was a fighter, protector, and could probably easily kick my ass.

I didn't know why I thought that was so hot.

And that was enough of that.

I looked in on her, took in every single cut and scrape and bruise, and nearly leaned down to brush my knuckle on the one finger that was outside of the blankets.

But I quickly pushed that thought from my mind, wondering why the urge had been there to begin with.

I shook my head and made my way back out of the infirmary to find Wilder standing on the other side of the door, his arms crossed over his massive chest.

"Did you get what you wanted?"

What did I want? I still didn't know why I had gone to check on her. I just needed to make sure she was there and actually okay. I needed to make sure London knew that her new friend and confidant was safe.

Or at least as safe as she could be in a place where she had been hurt. I was going to slaughter her attacker when I found him. And no mistake, I was going to find him.

"Yes. I can tell London that she's okay."

"And that's why you did it? To tell our baby sister that her new friend was going to be fine. Even though I could've done that myself?"

"As you said, she was hurt on our grounds. I'm pissed off. I might not like the woman, but I don't want to see her hurt. Let's figure out who the hell did this. I'm sure between her line of work and her attitude, she probably has a few enemies."

Wilder's jaw tensed. "You just can't help sniping at her, can you?"

"What can I say? It's what I do." I shrugged and grinned, quirking my lips in my patented smile, and Wilder just shook his head.

"I don't know why you try to pull that act on me when you know I can see right through it."

I snorted, grinning even harder. "You think you can? Whatever you say, spy boy. I'm way more mysterious than you give me credit for."

"Fine, big brother. You got a look at her. Now we're going to figure out why the hell that arsehole came after her."

I fisted my hands at my side for just a minute and then forced them to relax, telling myself that I was just furious because somebody was hurt on our grounds, not because Sparrow intrigued me... even if I disliked her.

"You do your job. You're good at it. I have work to do."

My brother studied my face. "As in an actual job? Papers Roman needs you to sign, or the set of twins I saw you talking to earlier today?"

I looked down at my fingernails and blew on them. "Well, I do have princely duties to fulfill since you and Roman seem to be acting like monks these days."

"One of these days, your dick is going to get you in trouble, Breck."

"I have royal dick. It's doing just fine."

"I'm pretty sure I heard Sparrow call you *the* royal dick, or *a* royal dick, so apparently, whatever title you just tried to bestow upon yourself backfired."

I shrugged. "I don't need Sparrow's approval. I'm sorry she's hurt, and I'm sure her team and you will figure it out. I have work to do."

Wilder muttered under his breath as I turned away from him. "Say hello to the twins."

I gave him a two-finger salute and made my way out of the infirmary. I sucked in a deep breath as soon as I walked outside, annoyed with myself for even bothering to check on her. I'd seen her when Wilder had picked her up and taken her away, and she'd been bloody and hurt. But Wilder had said it was just a small injury and they needed to keep her for observation. The fact that she was sleeping said they weren't worried about a concussion, or maybe I was wrong. I didn't know anything about head injuries.

I shook my head and made my way to my wing of our castle. To some people, it was odd to think that I had my own wing, or even lived in a castle, but it wasn't strange for me. I had grown up there.

Alden had always had a fairytale quality about it. It

was island off the coast of the United Kingdom, and we were a sovereign nation, our family having ruled for generations. When our parents died, my older brother had been crowned king, leaving me as the spare.

When I lost them, I also lost Roman in a way. The responsibility on his shoulders created this chasm between us.

I rubbed away the hurt at that thought, knowing I didn't need to venture too far into that territory. No amount of wallowing, crying, or praying was going to bring them back. No amount of being the perfect little prince would make me a better son in their eyes.

I loved my home and loved the people in it, even if they'd been quick to put the royal playboy title on me before I'd even lost my virginity. We'd all had labels thrown on us. I was the one who always smiled. Wilder was the one who tried to counter my free-spir-ited nature, and London, well, she was the pretty princess, and she'd had her share of labels put on her as well.

She had dealt with it finally, and was now a wife, soon to be mother, and had a career of her own that was outside the royal purview. It might annoy Roman that he couldn't keep her under his thumb and protected at all times, but she was thriving. I tried not to think about the fact that it was probably due in part to her husband,

Kannon, that she was thriving even more. Some things a brother didn't need to know.

When we were growing up, I had always been the one with the joke, the one who had tried his best to make people smile and laugh. After all, I was the spare, and for right now, the heir. I was second in line to the crown, and the only responsibility I had was not to shame the family name, though I might've tried it a few times. Our name could be tarnished, but never *truly* shamed. Roman did his best to make sure that never happened. My older brother, the king, was serious, a little dour, and pretty much an asshole. But I figured he had to be when he had the weight of a country on his shoulders, especially in a day and age when every country could watch him, judge him, and picture him in either perfection or in travesty.

Wilder had always been the quiet one, the serious one. While Roman might be serious with a perpetual need to dominate his world and keep it safe, Wilder had always been a little quieter about it, but no less fierce. Though every now and again, Wilder showed a little spirit.

I knew while Roman did his best to protect his family and country, Wilder was right there behind him, every step of the way, making sure that could indeed happen.

There was already enough seriousness in our family. They didn't need another grim-faced Waterford.

So I had stepped up to the plate as the superficial brother, and I couldn't help but have fun with it. After all, the royal playboy got to have a lot of fun, entertainment, and a never-ending supply of amusement.

I strolled past the courtyard and looked down onto the view from one of the terraces. The castle was set up amongst tall evergreen trees that looked gorgeous in winter with snow draped on them. I loved every piece of history within this stone, even if I knew some of it was shrouded in episodes that came from spilled royal blood.

The wind swept through my hair, and I pushed it from my face, closed my eyes, let out a breath, and just let myself be. After all, it wasn't often I felt free.

I HAD SLEPT LIKE SHIT. Instead of a blissfully dreamless sleep, my dreams had been filled with visions of satiny, honey-colored skin and dark eyes. Dark inky hair that cascaded over my pillow as I—well, never mind all that. The point was, Sparrow had made it impossible to get any rest. Not that I was worried about her or anything. Because that would be ridiculous.

And I knew I would feel that lack of rest before the

day ended. I had an appearance at a party later in the evening, and then I said I might stop by at a club opening on the other side of the city afterward. My name helped sell tickets to things, and I knew my worth, even if that worth sometimes changed day to day.

I had to be *on* for the rest of the day, and while I relished it, I knew I needed a little more pep before I was ready to play my public role.

"Prince Breck?" a low voice said from beside me, and I turned to see a woman with dark red hair piled on the top of her head. Her skin was pale and creamy with freckles dotted over her face. She had an Irish accent, thick curves, and a tiny waist. I wasn't quite sure how she could even walk in those heels of hers on the stone, but she was doing it just fine.

"Ah, Miss McKinney, is it?" I asked as she beamed at me.

"You're welcome to call me Siobhan."

I had zero intention of getting that familiar with her. However, when I smiled at her and a little blush swept over her cheeks, I smiled harder.

"What can I do for you?" I asked, almost offhandedly. She was beautiful and interested. Under normal circumstances, I'd already have steered her somewhere dark and private, but I had absolutely zero desire to do so. What the hell was wrong with me? A beautiful woman was smiling at me, giving me *I'm available* signals, and I didn't feel a damn thing.

"I was wondering if you were going to the event tonight?"

I went through my mental calendar to remember which one she was talking about and came up blank. "Ah, I have another engagement, but if you're going to be there, I may have to stop by."

"Oh, we would love you to."

And then another stunning beauty, the mirror image of the woman I was speaking with, joined us. "Yes, we would love you to come by."

They were the twins Wilder had spoken about. The twins that had a company ripe for acquisition. Because while they were there for a royal event, they were also co-CEOs of a major tech company in Ireland. And I had a vested interest in that. So, my job was to do what I did best.

Become the charming royal prince.

Instead of what was clearly on offer, all I could think about was the woman who hated me and was currently lying in a bed, hurt, bruised, and a shadow of herself.

"You know what, ladies? I will see you tonight at the event, but I need to check on something else right now."

They seemed a little disappointed, but I knew we

would talk business later. I would schmooze and smile, but I would not be sleeping with them.

Instead, I would be following up on our resident protector and figuring out who the hell had dared touch her.

Chapter 4
SPARROW

Change happens. It doesn't mean I have to like it.

ONE WEEK.

One week since some asshat had tried to tear my world down around me. One week since that jackhole had put his hands on me. The good news was the bruises had started to fade. The bad news was I fully intended to find the idiot and make him pay for trying to scare me.

You are *a little scared.*

No. Fear immobilized. Anger motivated. I needed to hold onto the lava-like rage flowing through my blood. Rage that some guy thought he could hurt me. Rage that I'd been so off my game. Rage that I'd been reckless.

Of all of this, what I hated the most was not trusting my instincts. I didn't make dumb mistakes.

Well, you do now.

No. I didn't. I just needed to get on my game. I would review every move, every turn, every choice, down to my new apartment, or flat as everyone called it in Alden. And when I found the chink in my armor, I'd fix it.

But this is the second time you've been attacked in less than six months.

I was not here for that particular brand of logic. I was aware that I was more tense than usual, but I refused to call that feeling fear.

I loved my flat. When I first saw it, I fell in love with its old-world charm and the stone and brick exterior, looking like something straight out of the 1800s as you came in the entrance. But it was a little dark in the building's entryway and could use better lighting.

But just up the narrow staircase and through my door was the brightest, most modern, beautiful space anywhere. Everything was light and airy and spacious. And the flat overlooked the gardens of the palace. It was only just around the corner from work, not at all far to the castle. And the best part was the cobblestones outside.

I loved everything that had old-world charm. But

now... now I regretted my choice. After Wilder and the doctor released me from my confines at the palace, my senses were too aware of the narrow stairway and the blind corners as it wound up to my floor. There were too many dark hallways and cubbies.

It screamed *not safe.*

And I hated that some asshole had stolen my joy like that.

As I started the morning, sipped my coffee, and enjoyed the sunshine over the gardens, I tried to tell myself I was making too much of it. I loved my apartment. I didn't want to give it up. It was even better than my apartment in LA, and that one was spectacular.

Then why are you afraid?

My phone chimed, and I glanced down at it. It was Kannon.

Kannon: *All good?*

Oh, Kannon. Ever loquacious. It was no wonder we'd gotten so tight. I'd learned right away that the best way to get him to talk about anything was to hammer him with questions constantly. Rapid fire. Eventually, he'd answer something. And sometimes I could repeat a question, and he'd finally answer it. Mostly to shut me up.

Somehow, he, of all people, had become my family. He looked out for all of us like we *were* family, which is why I wasn't going to let some little failed attempt at a mugging stop me from doing the best job that I could.

I had the personnel set up now. I had our equipment ordered. Everything was set up in the new office. Niko would be starting today. Olly, unfortunately, had to temporarily go back to LA and abandoned me—I was still bitter about that—to deal with our pressing case there. He'd be back in a month, but I was already feeling shorthanded. Not that he wanted to go, but when an A-lister requests you specifically after receiving threats, you've got to go. That left me feeling like I was on my own. I mean, Niko was great. He was sarcastic and funny. And we had a great time annoying Kannon. But Olly and I had built a tighter friendship than I had with Niko, which was probably why I felt his absence.

Niko also had this overprotective thing that he liked to do, which was annoying to say the least. So, he'd been shadowing my every move since the stupid attempted mugging. But he'd done me a solid and not ratted me out to Kannon, mostly because I'd let him mother-hen me to death. And he was holding it over me.

Why didn't he realize I was the damn boss? Not that that's how I wanted to play it. Niko was great at his job. And, if I was honest, I liked the fact that someone was looking out for me. Like I wasn't so alone. I hadn't wanted to tell Olly, but it had been a gut punch to find out he was going back. We'd both agreed to come to Alden together, and we worked well as a team. But it was what it was. I texted back.

Sparrow: *Fine. How's the vacation?*

Kannon: *You're chatty. It's fine. London is keeping me busy. Is everything okay with you?*

Sparrow: *Yup, everything is fine. The equipment showed up. Tech is setup. Niko is getting settled. Olly left for LA. But it's fine. It's not like we have any client files to get going yet.*

There was a beat before he replied. I got the impression that wasn't exactly the answer he expected.

Kannon: *I'm sure the office is fine. I'm asking how you are.*

I frowned at that. Not that Kannon wouldn't ask how I was, because he would. But I wondered if someone had ratted me out. I scowled as I was thinking about what Wilder might have said to him.

Or Breck. Thinking of him pulled my lip into an automatic sneer. I'd heard him when he'd come to see me. I'd been so foggy I couldn't respond, but I'd been listening. He'd been so irritated. What I didn't get was why? It's not like I knew him well. So why was he so annoyed with me? And honestly, he'd been more than a bit of a jackass, calling me an idiot for walking in the dark. He wasn't entirely wrong, but still.

I replied again, more aware of my words this time.

Sparrow: *All good. Seriously, enjoy your vacation. I have it handled here.*

Kannon: *I know you have it handled. I'm just checking in, making sure you're all good.*

Sparrow: *Yup, all good. Give London a hug for me. Tell me she owes me wine when she gets back.*

I stopped texting with him then. No way was I going to be late. I dressed quickly and was in the office in less than twenty minutes. Niko grinned at me from the kitchen and raised a cup of coffee. "You want one?"

I shook my head. "I already had one. How's it going?"

His grin was sheepish. "I know you told me to drop it, but just so you know, I combed through the security footage. I can't get a clear look at the guy who jumped you last week."

I groaned. "Jesus Christ, Niko, I told you not to."

"I know. It's just... You're my teammate, so I want to watch out for you."

"You know, I have someone else who does that too. His name is Kannon."

He grinned. "Boss-man likes to look out for you."

"Well, he's gone. For now, I'm the boss, and I don't want to waste resources. It was just a simple mugging."

Even as I said it, the words didn't ring true. But what

else could it have been? I didn't have any enemies. I hadn't been in Alden long enough to acquire any.

"Look, I hear you. I'd be up your ass too if you tried to babysit me. The thing is, I could only get so far. We're going to need someone who's better at tech to pull all the cameras from outside the palace. We have some access, but not enough."

I groaned. "What are the chances you're going to just let this go?"

Niko shrugged, making it clear that he intended to continue. His dark brows lowered. "I know you want to assume that it was a random attack. But you and the guy had a fight. And he *knew* how to fight. That doesn't worry you?"

Why did he have to speak sense? "It does, I guess. I just want to stop dwelling, get to work, and show Kannon that I can do this."

"Newsflash, Kannon already knows you can do this, and that's why you're in charge. That doesn't preclude you also taking care of yourself. Let's figure out who did this. Then we can open the new office, and we can all work on missions."

I rolled my eyes, but I knew he was right. I knew what I was going to do even before I walked into the office that morning. But the act of actually *doing* it, of asking for help, was the last thing I wanted.

I pulled my cellphone out of my purse, scrolled to Wilder's number, and then called. He answered on the first ring. "Hey, Sparrow, how are you feeling?"

I sighed. "I'd be so much better if that wasn't the first question everyone asks me."

"Sorry, that would make me nuts too."

"Thank you. But I'm fine. Listen, I think I need your help going through the footage of my attack. We need access to all of Alden's security feeds, public and private, if possible. Anything with a lead."

"Sure thing. Why don't you head to the palace now? I can give you a hand and get you access before I have my eleven o-clock. Does that sound good?"

I sighed. "Yup, sounds great."

I hung up with him and grabbed my purse again. "Niko, I'm going up to the palace."

Niko just grunted from his office. "You're spending an awful lot of time up there. You and Prince Wilder about to do the horizontal mambo?"

I rolled my eyes. "No. Believe it or not, we're friends. And I like him. But major brother vibes there."

He chuckled. "Only you would look at a prince like a brother."

"It's accurate." I shrugged.

He sighed like he was my long-suffering mother

attempting to marry me off. "But you *never* see anyone as someone to shag, do you?"

"Not entirely true." But the one person that made my blood boil was on the *Do Not Bone* list. I wrinkled my nose at him as he leaned his head out so that I could see him in the doorway.

"So, what you're saying is that all my careful attempts to seduce you are failing?"

I shrugged. "You're not trying very hard."

He laughed. "Man, you couldn't even handle it if I stepped up my game."

"Step up your game. Let's see it."

He rolled his eyes. "I'm telling you; you couldn't handle my game."

I laughed as I swung my bag over my shoulder. "If you say so. I'll see you later."

Normally, I would have opted to walk. But who knew how long I would be at the palace? I didn't think walking back to the office would be the best choice after sundown. But this time, I parked right in front of the guard tower. It was impossible to miss, brightly lit, right under a light.

I wouldn't be caught unaware again.

I showed my ID at the main entrance of the palace, and I was in front of Wilder's office door in no time.

When I knocked, he opened the door and scrutinized me. "Are you sure you're okay?"

I sighed. "I swear to God."

He put his hands up. "Okay, okay. Have a seat. Tell me what you need."

"Well, access to palace security feeds. Niko has been looking, but he's no Olly. He tried to tap into the businesses on the outer perimeter of the palace in the surrounding neighborhoods. He's being insistent, just in case this wasn't random."

Wilder frowned and then sat on the edge of his desk as he watched me. "All right. I can help get you access, but someone should go through them with you. And unfortunately, that can't be me. I've got a hell of a day. The rest of the week is not looking better, either."

"No, it's fine. If you can give me access, I can do it myself."

Slowly, he shook his head. "Look, I don't like this. I personally think you need to stay in the palace." Even as I shook my head, he added, "But I know that's not going to happen."

"It's not."

"Well, I could force it."

I scowled. "No, thanks. I'm not one of your subjects, remember?"

He sighed. "All right, fine. That's why I'm not insisting. But listen, I think it's for the best."

"And when I agree with you, I will do that."

"Fine. Then please, accept my other offer of help."

I watched him warily. "What do you mean by other *offer?*"

"Well, you need security cam access, right?"

"That would be great. If there's that much of it to sort through, I'll pull Niko off his other stuff and we can—"

He laughed. "Um, I'm going to do even better than Niko."

He typed something quickly on his phone, and in a few seconds, there was a knock at his door.

"Come in."

I turned slowly. Then I froze.

Breck.

There was just something about his presence that always sent my body into a hyper-aware state, like I was poised to run. Like I didn't know what the safest course of action was. Run and hide, or stay and stare.

Breck scowled when he saw me too. "What is she doing here? Isn't she supposed to be convalescing somewhere?"

I rolled my eyes and turned my back to him. It was only when I met Wilder's eyes that I understood what was happening here. He'd meant that Breck was the help I was supposed to accept.

I shook my head. "No. You can't be serious."

Wilder smiled. "Look, big brother here is the tech genius anyway. It will take you significantly less time to search, and he already has a head start. Just accept the help."

I scowled at him. No matter how hard I tried, it seemed I couldn't get away from Breck Waterford.

Chapter 5

BRECK

Hate to love only works when it's not me.

SON OF A BITCH.

Why the hell did Wilder want me in the same room as her? Did he have a death wish? Because I had a feeling Sparrow was one joke away from killing us both.

Which is why I had to say it. Anything to keep her away from me and get me out of that damn confining room.

"Sparrow, darling, if you wanted to get in my royal pants, all you had to do was ask. And while I'm up for threesomes," I gave Wild a pointed look and ignored his warning glare, "I'm not up for bedding you with my brother. There are some royal swords one mustn't cross."

Sparrow just blinked at me, those beautiful eyes of hers going wide and taking up more real estate on her face.

Wilder's response was more predictable. "Damn it, Breck," he snapped.

I raised a brow. "What? All I'm saying is I'm not going to have a threesome with you. That is why you asked me to come here, right?" I was in a surly mood after the week I'd had. Seeing Sparrow and tormenting her just a little normally would have cheered me up, but being summoned by my brother was putting a damper on my joy.

Dealing with the CEOs of the companies I was trying to acquire this week had exhausted me, and not in any fun way. They were sharks when it came to business, and they had kept me second-guessing my promise when it came to strategy and tech.

I hadn't slept much, and I wasn't going to pretend it was only because of that. When I closed my eyes, I could see the bruises on Sparrow's face. And in my waking hours, I was reminded of them when I saw her around the palace. They weren't as dark as they were in my dreams, but they were still there.

And damn it, I didn't want to think about that. Or

her. Or her scent. Or the way her teeth grazed her bottom lip when she was irritated.

"Him?" Sparrow asked, her voice low and incredulous. "You can't be serious, Wild. You know this is a bad idea." She pursed her lips, broadcasting her displeasure for me like a bloody billboard. "We, uh, won't work well together. While I appreciate your help, I think I'm better off on my own."

"Sparrow," Wilder began.

She held her hand up, and Wilder snapped his jaw shut. Interesting. I rarely could get that to happen. What kind of power did she wield over him? "Honestly, I appreciate it. But I'm sure His Royal Highness doesn't want to work with me either."

"And by 'His Royal Highness,' I'm sure you mean Playboy Fuck-up. But I suppose that's better than Fuckboy Prince."

She sent me a glower and muttered something along the lines of "You said it. I didn't," before resuming her attempt to wiggle out of my help. "I'm sure the prince has, erm, better things to do than figure out who came onto your grounds and tried to mug me."

She had to be kidding. My brows rose to my hairline. "Mugging? You're calling it a mugging? The guy that came at you did it with skill and determination, and you're going to play it like it was a simple mugging. *In Alden?*"

The look she gave me could wither a man's balls. I nearly took a step back but realized that would look weak, and I wasn't about to have that happen.

"It *was* a mugging. At least that's what we're going with for now," Sparrow added. "I need access to the system so I can check out where he came from exactly and where he went when he escaped. I'm new in Alden, so I don't have enemies or anything. So why pick me as a target and not take anything? I obviously can't find him if I don't have full access to the security systems and a couple of hands to help search. And without Olly here, Niko and I, while we are clearly able to do it, needed a little help. However, since it seems you're busy," she said, "I don't want to put anyone out. Niko and I can figure it out all by ourselves."

She tried to brush past me, but I slid smoothly into her path, putting myself between her and the door.

"I'm sure your *friend* Niko is very talented," I purred, and she narrowed her eyes into slits. "Only he's not as talented as me. That is, *if* I decide to help."

She lifted her chin and glowered at me, and my dick hardened. Motherfucking hell. *Down boy.* She seemed like a viper more likely to bite my dick off than make it feel good. And as gorgeous as she was to look at, she was not my type.

I loved to see her move. The sexy sway of her ass had commanded my attention more than once. She was smart as a tack, and I loved to watch her work. Hell, I could even respect her, but I wanted nothing to do with her. She wouldn't be a quick fuck, and that's all I wanted in life. No, Sparrow was the kind of woman you kept. Therefore, she wasn't the one for me.

But somebody needed to tell that to my dick.

Not to mention she was a friend of my sister's, and London would kill me if I dared touch a friend of hers. Yet hell, just her looking at me like that? It took me a second to calm myself. The last thing I needed was her knowing that I got hard every time she was around me.

"So, you're going to do it then, Breck?" Wilder asked, and I turned my head away from Sparrow, breaking the connection that was probably only on my side.

What the hell did he just ask me? "Do what?"

Sparrow whirled away from me and faced my brother. "See, Wilder? He can't even pay attention for two seconds, and you think he's going to be able to help me find who attacked me?" She sighed. "Look, Breck, I'm sure you're good at what ever princely thing you do, but I need someone I can actually count on. And I respect you, Wilder, but I need to ensure this is dealt with and Kannon Security is safe before Kannon and London get back. And I can't do that with him," she said, pointing at me over her shoulder.

There was something about her tone that said she wasn't trying to hurt me to be malicious, even though she knew exactly where to hit me. I was used to the reputation, used to people thinking that I was the flake, that I was third best, not even worthy of being second best.

And that was usually fine.

I didn't like the fact that *she* felt that way, though.

"You two need to stop acting like children and talk to each other. Breck is the best when it comes to tech. He could probably rival your Olly."

I nearly puffed out my chest at that compliment, but held back at Sparrow's look.

"Please, nobody's as good as Olly. No need to put yourselves out. Niko and I are good on our own."

I ignored the barb. But this was the second time she'd mentioned Niko. It made me wonder who this Niko was to her. But it wasn't any of my business. She could be with who she wanted. I shouldn't care. And yet, I did. And I hated it.

"I need you to pull it together and stop acting like first years. I know you guys seem to piss each other off just by breathing, but get over it." Wilder practically growled. "I will get Roman involved if I must, so don't push me."

I held back a curse. Roman intervening would be a headache. I loved my brother, but he could be a tyrant. That's what happened when your brother was a king.

"I'm not Your Highness's royal subject," Sparrow muttered.

"Oh, I'm fully aware of that, but you were hurt on our grounds, and I want to know why."

"So do I," I added, dropping the attitude for a moment.

Sparrow shot me a look. "I would just rather not have Breck helping."

Wilder's voice was soft as he addressed her. "I want to make sure it's not going to happen again, and it's not part of something bigger. Because not only do I want our people to stay safe, London and Kannon will be back eventually, and if anyone dares harm a hair on my baby sister's head, there'll be hell to pay. Breck is the fastest way to that solution."

Sparrow's eyes softened for a moment, and then they nearly blinked in surprise. Well, it seemed caring about my sister was a way to soften her on the idea of me.

"Trust me, I'm as unhappy as you are, but the faster

I help you, the faster I'll be out of your hair. Come with me to my office," I said after a minute.

"Said the spider to the fly," she muttered.

"I promise not to eat you," I said with a grin.

"Wild," Sparrow pleaded.

"Go." He looked at me. "And stop acting like you're twelve, Breck," Wilder muttered.

"I wasn't this bad when I was twelve," I said. "Or maybe I was worse, mostly because I didn't have the full vocabulary of the fiend that I am now."

I winked and then turned on my heel, grateful when she followed me.

"Where is your office?" she asked, annoyed.

"I have a home office here, I also have one in another building, but let's not bother driving there."

"You mean an actual office? Not just your bedroom with the velvet sheets?" Sparrow asked sarcastically.

And now there was an image of Sparrow draped on black velvet, or perhaps even black silk, her hair strewn about her, her skin kissed by the soft light.

I'd spread her thighs, slowly bite my way up her silkiness, before licking that sweet honey, one taste, one touch until she came on my mouth, and I drove her to orgasm.

And then I'd sink my cock inside her, watch as she arched for me, her breasts right in my face as I licked and I sucked, and I fucked her hard into those velvet sheets.

Or were they silk?

Get your shit together. Sparrow isn't like that. Stop with the fantasy.

Sparrow eyed me warily. She was right to be wary. I wasn't to be trusted. I cleared my throat, wishing my cock would stop pressing so hard against my slacks.

I was probably going to hell, but damn, I was sure having fun on my way down there.

In my office she glanced around, brows raised as she practically tripped into the room. "Dear God," she muttered.

I had screens on one side of the wall, arching to the other side, tables with other tablets, and tech in the center. There were electronic boards on the opposite wall. That way, I could work out what I was thinking there, and automatically go directly to my server, and I could look at my computer instead of recoding everything.

I was good at making tech, fucking brilliant at math, and I was okay at security. Wilder was better, or I'd call myself great.

"What is all this?"

"It's my porn kingdom. How do you think I edit all

those videos?" The joke fell flat, and she just stared at me and shook her head.

"Who are you?" she asked, her voice barely above a whisper.

I swallowed hard and pushed my dirty thoughts from my head. "I am who I need to be. I've already been looking up some of the footage, and I'm trying to find out where he got in. There's a hole in our security system, and I think it has to do with the IDs."

"You've already been looking?" Sparrow asked as she came to my side and pulled out her tablet. "I should bring Niko in on this."

My shoulders tensed, and I shook my head. "He can meet us in my other office once we get some things done. Let's get through this initial stuff, and you tell me what you need, and I'll get it to you. That way, you can get back to your job, and I can do mine."

Because I couldn't do anything while she was sitting in my space, making it smell like her, like fresh linen, almost like ocean water, clean. It was too much, even more so than if it had been floral or fruity. It was just Sparrow.

And it made me want to lick that honey-brown skin and pull at that dark hair of hers to move her head just a bit so I could latch onto her neck and suck.

I was turning into a bloody vampire, and I had no idea why.

"This is what I need," Sparrow said, naming off a bunch of specs.

"Drop it in the cloud that I'm sending you the link for," I said, tapping a few keys on a computer.

Sparrow's eyes widened at my set up, but I pushed her to the side mentally, getting into the zone.

"I'll get you what you need, and then we'll work on the back angles because I'm a little worried."

"Worried?" she asked, and I nearly cursed. I hadn't meant to say that.

"After Aunt Rebecca, it's been tense around here. Trusting the wrong people will make you wary."

Sparrow winced. "I'm sorry. I know she practically raised you guys. It must've been hard to have her turn on you like that."

I shrugged like it didn't matter, even though it sure as fuck did. "Nothing we can do about it now. Everybody shows their true face eventually, we were just almost a little too late to realize it." I paused, pushing back the anger. "Plus, she mostly raised London."

"And who raised you?"

I shrugged again, focusing on my work as I moved through files. "I had mom and dad longer."

I could practically see her doing the math.

"Maybe not as long as Roman, but I had them longer than Wilder and London. So that's all that matters. Plus, Roman was always there for us. In the end, we only needed each other. And eventually I only needed myself."

We were silent for so long that I was afraid I had said too much. Fuck, I knew I was revealing too much. I didn't know what it was about Sparrow, but she ruffled my feathers, and I couldn't focus.

Finally, Sparrow cleared her throat. "I guess I should head back and meet up with Niko while you get me what I need." She gave me a look that told me she didn't think I could do it.

I ground my teeth. "Niko, right. Run along now." I said, trying to push the boundaries again. I didn't like her getting so close. It annoyed me. And I was fucking lying to myself.

She glared at me. "And you know what? You're so much more palatable when you're not talking. Get me the specs, and thank you, what was that you called yourself? Oh yes, Fuckboy Prince." She strode out of my office, leaving behind that damn scent.

And every mistake I knew I was going to make.

Chapter 6
BRECK

The black sheep of the family waves hello.

I PROBABLY SHOULD HAVE SLEPT the night before, but I figured I'd functioned on less sleep in my life. Usually it was because of far more pleasant experiences, but not so much recently, since I was diving into my new projects. There was probably something wrong with me if I wanted to spend the night with my computers rather than a willing woman, but times change, and sometimes a man needed a break.

What I needed was more sleep, but since I knew that wasn't going to happen, I went with more coffee— the sweet elixir of life and keeping this prince awake.

I chugged down the last of my coffee, grateful nobody was there to watch me. Years of etiquette classes, though maybe not as many as London, had instilled me to be slow and deliberate with my actions.

I had chucked that idea out the window as soon as I could.

Much to my teachers' and family's chagrin.

I considered another cup, but I figured my brothers would probably have some waiting for me. After all, they were the ones that had set this meeting. They were going to have to deal with me and all of my grumpiness. They were used to it.

I grunted, ran my hand through my hair, and thought I should probably shower. However, I had taken a shower at around midnight, trying to reinvigorate my brain. I always did my best thinking in the shower and had even developed a voice app to help me write down notes while I was showering. I used to use those water-proof notepads, but I was a techie at heart and liked creating my things.

That little app had created a nice amount of pocket change. I'd donated most of what I made off the sale to my favorite charities, and the anonymous donation had helped fund a few schools. I obviously didn't need the money. But it was nice I was still getting letters from the children who wanted to say thank you, even if they didn't know my name. The fact that London regularly visited some of those schools around the world always made me smile, even if she didn't know I was the one that had built them.

I pushed those thoughts from my mind and made my way to Roman's wing.

Best not to be late since I had been summoned.

When the king called, I answered.

Usually.

I nodded at a few of the staff members as they shuffled past, each of them on a mission of their own, diligent, but happy. I liked the feel of the house now, not that it had ever been off before. Yet, now that Aunt Rebecca was gone, I realized there was less tension in the air. As if she had been the one pushing everybody to work just a little past their abilities, or even worse, setting unrealistic expectations for the staff.

Nothing like having your aunt turn out to be a homicidal murderer to shed some light on a few things.

I knew the Council of Lords tended to do that independently, but Aunt Rebecca seemed to take things to a whole new level. But she was no longer here, much to my disappointment. I didn't want her anywhere near my family, but I would have liked to have said a few words to her before she'd been taken away. I wanted to tell her exactly what I thought of her and make sure she knew that she would never see London again.

My heart went full jackrabbit in my chest, and my hands fisted. *Hell.* I let out a slow breath, annoyed I'd let those thoughts filter in.

"It's about time you showed up," Roman said as I strolled into his set of suites. We were in the foyer where there were a few ornate chairs and tables strewn about. The draperies had been pulled back, showcasing the high ceilings and elegant molding. Sunlight streamed in, and there was a direct view to the balcony and then the king's garden beyond. Through the door on the right was the war room then the bedrooms. Over to the left was a fully appointed chef's kitchen and dining room should Roman want to show off his culinary skills.

He sometimes met dignitaries or had council meetings here. He didn't usually host family here, but when I realized that I had been summoned for something that wasn't necessarily family related, it made sense.

The fact that Roman was facing the window, looking over his vast kingdom that he ruled with a decently iron fist, or maybe more with an iron open palm, made me wonder how he had seen me without even looking at me. Maybe it was the reflection, or maybe he was just that good when it came to sensing the presence of others.

"Sorry, late morning," I said, purposely yawning wide and searching the room for coffee. I grinned as I saw the ornate coffee setup and sauntered over to it, scratching my belly as I did. Wilder rolled his eyes and shook his head.

"Really?" he muttered.

"What? I just woke up."

A lie, but I had just rolled out of my chair, so that was almost the same thing.

I had projects to complete, people counting on me, and I needed to find out who might be after Sparrow. Or our family.

"If you're awake now," Roman drawled, "it's time for us to discuss what happened here."

I bit into one of the pastries chef had made and nearly groaned. "Don't mind me. I'm just orgasming over cream cheese."

Roman rolled his eyes and turned to meet my gaze. "You know, you're not getting any younger. You're the heir; you need to stop acting like you're just a spare."

No way I was touching that ticking time bomb. "So, why did you summon us?" I asked. "Is it just us?"

"No, we're here too," a familiar voice said from behind me, and I turned to see London and her husband Kannon on the screen.

My eyes widened, and I grinned, this time with sincerity. "Well, hello there, baby sister. And Kannon."

My brother-in-law narrowed his eyes at me. "Breck. I see you're up to your usual shenanigans."

"You know, I love the word shenanigans. We don't use it enough these days."

"I'm sure we use it enough around you," London said, beaming. London knew me pretty well, and though I liked to pretend I was the laughing brother who would always make her smile, I was just as overprotective of her as Wilder and Roman. Maybe more sometimes because I tended to surprise her when I did it, but she just needed to get used to it.

"Anyway, now that we're all here, let's get started," Wilder said, clearing his throat.

I swallowed the rest of my Danish, downed the last of my coffee, and set everything to the side. I wiped my hands on the linen napkin and then poured myself a glass of water. Everyone stood in silence as they watched me, and I nearly groaned. I was starving, thirsty, and in desperate need of caffeine. It wasn't my fault that everything I needed just happened to be right there in front of me. They could talk around me.

"We're here to discuss Sparrow and the attack."

I swallowed a gulp of water and nodded. "I sent over

the specs to Wild and Sparrow and her team." I turned to Kannon. "Did you see?"

Kannon gave me a tight nod. "Yes. I saw. And we're still going to be looking at exactly what happened."

"Yes, you're going to need to work with Sparrow a bit longer because Olly's not here since they're setting up the other team in California," Wilder said.

I nodded. "I can do that," I said, trying to sound professional. Although, I didn't know if anybody believed me.

"Why exactly are we forcing these two people to work together?" Kannon asked Wilder instead of me.

I swallowed hard, trying not to think about why Roman wouldn't trust me to make these kind of decisions. I hadn't done anything to take away that trust, but it was just easier to step away and let Wilder act like the heir, the protector, while I did what I needed to do. I partied harder, I smiled more, and I felt like I could never live up to what Roman needed me to be. So I didn't. I did my own thing outside the family purview. And that was just fine with me. They didn't need to know about my tech or my company. They didn't need to know the long hours I worked. Because it wasn't for the family, so what good was it? It was just mine. Something that could be mine for the first time in, well, I didn't want to think about that.

I shook my head, annoyed with myself for even thinking about stuff like that. I didn't need to wallow in my misery while they were discussing Sparrow and Kannon's teams in California and here in Alden. I needed to focus on them, and yet I could only focus on the way that Roman leaned on Wilder, and now on Kannon, and I was the odd man out.

Roman was always overprotective when it came to London, so it made sense that he wouldn't lean on her, even though she would always be there to step in when needed. But me? I was just there to cut ribbons and kiss babies, just like Sparrow had said before.

And I needed to stop thinking about Sparrow. We were two completely different people, and me thinking about her in any way other than as the annoying new person on security was a bad call. Not only was she my sister's friend who worked with the palace at times, she was the forever type. It was written all over her face. You didn't screw around with that. And I could not make that mistake, yet I had a feeling if I wasn't careful, I was going to do what I did well. Make another fucking error.

"Are you done wool-gathering and finally ready to listen?" Roman asked.

I swallowed hard. "Sorry, I didn't sleep much."

Roman narrowed his eyes, but Wilder looked nonplussed.

"Just keep working with her. I have a weird feeling that this is only the beginning," Wilder said.

Chills washed over me, and I nodded tightly, my chin raised. "I've got it. I'll fill in and cover whatever Olly can't do from where he is."

"And we can get on a flight right back to Alden," Kannon said, and London nodded. "Really. We can be there to help."

As if they didn't trust me to do it myself. Well, I would just have to show all of them. I cleared my throat. "I've got it. You don't need to watch out for little Sparrow. Not only could she probably kick anyone's ass and take care of herself, I'll be there to help."

I ignored the disbelief on everyone's faces.

I was the one who had put it out there to begin with, and now I was going to have to deal with the consequences.

"IF YOU KEEP FROWNING at the screen, your eyes will cross."

I blinked, uncrossed my eyes, and looked over at Jaye. "What?"

"You hadn't blinked in a full minute, and your eyes are going to dry out. Plus, you have this frown on your face that makes me believe you are either thinking too hard or you're not thinking about the topic at hand."

I shook my head, embarrassed. I didn't usually slack off at work—even if most people wouldn't believe it. I usually had my head down, focusing on the projects at hand and what we could be doing better on our next assignments. I had a team that worked for me and relied on me to be the boss—not the prince most people saw.

And clearly, I wasn't doing a good enough job of it right then. "I'm fine. Stop staring at me. And if you're studying my face enough to notice when I'm blinking, you're not paying attention to your task."

Jaye rolled her eyes. "True, true. Okay, if you're not going to focus on the work in front of you, can you help me look at this code?"

I nodded at two other team members who were in our office as I walked over to her. We all liked to work in a community setting rather than telecommuting from home. My goal was for everyone to be able to work where they were more comfortable as long as they could keep up with the steady and fast pace of the team. Another of our programmers was on maternity leave but kept trying to email work in as if I didn't know she was exhausted from lack of sleep and covered in baby drool.

Or whatever else babies excreted. We'd all kindly reminded her that she didn't have to check in and be present if she didn't want to, and her job would be there when she was ready to come back. I valued each and every person on my team, and I'd do whatever I could to make them comfortable. The more freedom they had, the better work they created.

"What do you need?" I asked as I took a seat next to Jaye's workstation.

"There's something wrong with this code, and it's frustrating me. See?" She clicked a few keys, and I nodded along, noting what she'd added since we'd last talked. "Not that the code is wrong, per se, but we're at the troubleshooting part of the process, and I think I've added too much trouble." She went on in detail about the issues, and I nodded again then started taking notes.

"I think I see the problem."

She rolled her eyes. "Of course, you do. One minute at my computer and, boom, you understand what I haven't been able to work out in the last three hours."

I laughed, shaking my head. "No, that's not it. You've been looking at this same code for three hours, but I'm coming at it from a fresh viewpoint. And I recognize a mistake I made myself on another project. One that isn't really a mistake, but something that tends to wrap around itself and confuse anyone who has any semblance of coding language." I gestured toward her keyboard. "May I?"

She nodded. "Have at it. I might start growling at this point."

"That would be a change of pace," I said in a deadpan tone, and she snorted. I typed a few notes and made a few suggestions but didn't alter her code. "Start from here and see if that works itself out. If not, then we'll play around with it a bit more."

Her nose scrunched as she studied the read out. "If that's the issue, I'm going to bang my head against my desk."

"Feel free. I still have a dent from where I did the same thing."

She grinned. "The one on your head? Or on your desk?"

I rolled my eyes, then went back to my office to work on a few things on my list for the day. I wasn't behind, but I was going to be if I didn't keep up with my pace. Only, my mind wasn't on work—something that wasn't usual for me.

Instead, it was on a woman I shouldn't want. A woman that could be in danger.

And I had no idea what to do about it.

Chapter 7
SPARROW

Sparks fly, and they tend to burn.

IT HAD BEEN two days since I'd last spoken to Breck, and while he had sent a few emails over to Niko, I didn't even know if he was genuinely working on the problem at all. And honestly, I had to put everything on the back burner. It had to have just been a mugging, a crime of opportunity.

Except he didn't actually mug you.

That little voice wouldn't leave me alone. I'd been over that day dozens of times in my head. There was something off, but I couldn't put my finger on it. I had to let it go for the moment though. I had a job to do. And as the acting boss of Kannon Security, I needed to be on top of my game. I needed to stop focusing on that niggling voice and worry about Kannon Security. We had a lot more to do than following up on what had happened to me.

Mainly finishing setting up our new ancillary office after Kannon married London and decided he wanted to live in the country where she was a member of the monarchy. Our group was like a family. We worked hard and always had each other's backs. And not everybody needed to move to Alden and work on the international branch of our division. We were used to travelling the world often to be bodyguards and perform other security functions for spoiled rich girls, diplomats, and royalty when they visited other countries. And we were good at our jobs. In fact, we had been on a job in Paris when we had first come upon London, and she had been running for her life. Even if she hadn't realized it, it was quite dramatic at the time.

And when Kannon had decided to move here permanently, as his number two, I'd come with him. I didn't have much to tie me down back home, and I had fallen in love with Alden. It spoke to me in a way that I hadn't planned on. I also wanted to make sure someone had Kannon's back, and it might as well be me. Besides, I could work just as well here as in California. And

Alden was closer to Mauritius than Los Angeles was. So it was the matter of one flight if I wanted to see my family.

We had brought Niko and Olly with us, but Olly had gone back to the States to wrap up training of new team members, including his replacement as the California tech guru. And since Olly was even more anal-retentive than I was when it came to our positions, it made sense that he had gone back to finish up.

Under normal circumstances, he could work on all the Alden assignments from California until he was ready, but since this had to do with royal security and systems that he couldn't get into from the outside, at least not legally, that meant we'd had to ask for help. *Breck. He who shall not be thought about.*

Though that was easier said than done.

Niko had volunteered to come over too, and he was the perfect addition. He was our second string when it came to medical as well, since Max had family obligations and had stayed at the California office.

So for now, we were a small team of four in Alden with the others remaining in California, but they could and would meet us wherever there was a job. We were two prongs of a very efficient system, and for now, I was at the helm.

It shouldn't feel weird to me, except for the fact that

Kannon never took a vacation. Not ever. So while I was number two, I'd rarely been given the chance to lead the team. I knew the guys trusted me as second, but now I felt like I needed to prove to both myself and the guys that I was the right choice to run the team in Alden.

And if I said that to any one of them, they'd roll their eyes, laugh at me, and say I was an idiot for questioning them.

But I couldn't help my thoughts. I always needed to prove myself.

"What's wrong with your face? It's doing this frowny thing like you're contemplating who to kill." Niko asked as he looked over his case file.

"Just thinking, and it's pissing me off. Where is Mr. Prince?" I asked, my tone full of snark. "He's the one who demanded we meet him here." I was surprised not to be meeting at the palace or at Kannon Security. Instead, Breck had had us come to his office, which was much different than I thought it would be. It was more tasteful than I pictured. Sure there was glass and chrome, but there was also elegant design. The art on the walls was modern, and somehow, despite all the glass, the office interior managed to appear warm and exuded effortless cool.

Niko raised a brow as we were led to Breck's office by a lithe blonde who exuded a no-bullshit air. "Wow.

And the prince, he's not so bad. I kind of like the guy. I don't know why he's always getting under your skin."

I flipped him off as I spun around in one of the fancy chairs. "I don't think he likes you, so you shouldn't like him. Not that there's much to like."

Niko snorted. "That's not what I hear around the palace. Everyone likes him. They don't think much of him beyond being the second son, but they like him."

Niko had this way of seeing what wasn't said. So I was curious what he thought of Breck. "What do you mean?"

Niko shrugged. "There are some who think he hasn't lived up to his potential or wish he would get a real job or something, but I think they're just jealous. And maybe they haven't seen this place."

"Jealous of what?"

Niko met my gaze. "Jealous of the power he wields probably. He's second in line to the throne. You may think he's throwing it all away by smiling too much and flirting with anything with legs, but you still have to respect the guy for coming in and helping us. He did send over some good info." He whistled low. "And look at this place. It's a tech nerd heaven in here."

I let out a little growl. "Don't get blinded by the trappings. And that information was probably easy to find. We just didn't have access. He's not being helpful; he's throwing us a bone."

"Did someone say something about a bone?" the man of the hour asked as he strolled in through the office door. I resisted the urge to roll my eyes, but just barely.

Niko lifted his chin over at the prince. "Hey, we were just talking about you."

"Dirty things I hope," he said, winking.

Damn it. I hated it when he winked. *Liar.*

Breck cleared his throat and took a step to the side as an Asian woman behind him stepped out from his shadow and smiled. Her inky dark hair hung to her waist, and her sharp, shrewd eyes were a warm cocoa. "Hi, everyone."

"This is Jaye. She works with me, and I like to say she is the brains of the operation."

Well, that just made more sense. This poor woman probably worked her ass off while he took all the credit.

Jaye just smiled. "Sure, I'm totally the brains." She waved awkwardly. "Anyway, I'm going to go take a seat over here out of the way while we wait to hear from Olly."

She practically bounced as she made her way to the chair, and I met Breck's gaze. "What was that about?" I whispered, and Niko moved closer to listen in.

Breck bent forward just slightly, his aftershave tickling my senses, and I tried my best to ignore it. How could I already feel the heat of him so close? Damn the man.

"I think she has a crush on our dear Olly's... *talents.* I don't know about the man himself, but we hear things in our circles."

I blinked in surprise. "Your circles?"

Breck's face blanked, and it looked like he thought he'd said too much. But what the hell was he talking about?

"Anyway, will Olly be on soon? We have things to do. And I'm sure you have people to arrest, or guard, or whatever it is you do." He took a seat by Jaye and pulled out an unusual-looking tablet. His fingers worked across the front of it quickly, smoothly, as if he wasn't just playing on social media but doing something important.

I frowned as I looked over at the tablet and tilted my head. "What is that?"

He looked up with barely a glance before looking back down at his hands. "It's a prototype hearing aid. The heritage trust commissioned one to help some of our elderly and hearing-impaired residents. Ones currently on the market are often times too big and the small ones too costly. So I came up with a cost-effective alternative. We're working out all the kinks now, but hopefully we can get it on the market soon."

"Market?" I asked, confused.

"It's tech. It's what I do. Build tech to make our everyday lives easier. Sometimes apps too. I don't just code you know."

"Who are you?" I whispered, and I didn't even realize I'd said it out loud until Niko snorted beside me.

I glared at him, and then he gave me a sweet and innocent face as the comm chimed.

Niko pressed the button, and Olly's face filled the screen. His eyes looked tired, but he gave us a smile nonetheless. "Hey there, everyone. Sorry I'm late. We had an issue, but we're set up now."

I went on alert, my shoulders tense. "Issue?"

"An 'I was locked out of the office' issue," Olly said, his cheeks red.

Niko burst out laughing as Breck gave me an inquisitive look, and I felt forced to answer.

"Our dear Olly is brilliant behind the scenes on the computer and decent at other aspects of his job relating to security. However, picking a lock to get back into a room? Well, we're not going to talk about the Toronto incident."

"I thought we agreed to never mention the Toronto incident," Olly said, his cheeks going even redder.

"I'm not the one that brought it up," Niko said, his hands up in the air in a defensive position.

"Okay, enough of that," I said, my lips twitching. For some reason, I met Breck's gaze, and he smiled at me. That did things to me, warm things. Very low. I did not want to think about that. I *couldn't* think about that.

I cleared my throat. "Olly, this is Jaye. She works with Breck. I think."

"Oh, I've heard of you. You guys at Royal Water Tech have been doing some great things. I like your work."

Jaye sputtered, and I just sat there, confused.

"Royal Water?" I asked.

"Don't worry about it. Silly thing, just a game," Breck said, waving me off.

I looked over at Olly, whose eyes widened fractionally, but he just pressed his lips together and nodded tightly. "Got it. Anyway, I can't wait to get there and work on my setup. It feels weird doing everything here when I don't even have my station set up in the office. We've been a little busy on this end, with all the extra weddings and babies and jobs we've been taking."

Breck frowned and looked down at his tablet again. "When you get back, we can talk. I have a few ideas for where you can set up that will be better for the network and will give you easier access to things that you might need. I don't know about the whole security issue other than how to be the guy the bodyguard protects, but I think you and I can get along," Breck said, surprising me.

Olly's eyes widened, excitement running through him. "Oh, I like you.

"You know, I think that's flirting in geek-speak," Niko said, and Olly blushed again while Jaye sputtered and Breck just let out a low rumbling laugh that went straight through me.

What was it about this man? I had no idea who *this* Breck Waterford was, but he was *not* the guy that I talked to, day in and day out. Was he a doppel-gänger? An evil twin? No, the royal pain in my ass would be the evil twin. This would be the good twin they hid in the dungeon who just showed up every once in a while for meetings or to confuse the fuck out of me.

"Anyway, what do you need today?" Breck asked.

I tensed. "Excuse me?"

"You said you needed a meeting. I assume you have notes? Or are you just here to gaze upon my pretty face?"

Niko whistled under his breath, and Olly turned slightly and started talking to Jaye. The two of them spoke in geek-speak that I couldn't quite understand. I just narrowed my eyes at the prince. Was he trying to get under my skin? I didn't understand. He was getting along with everyone else but apparently had to be an asshole to me.

I cleared my throat. "Do you mind coming outside for a minute? I think you and I need to have a conversation."

"It seems I have a meeting with the teacher," he said, and set his tablet on his chair as he stood up. "I'll be right back. Don't have too much fun while I'm gone," he said, winking, acting like the normal self. The evil self.

Where had the good twin gone?

I stormed out of the room, my chest heaving, and I didn't understand why. He hadn't said anything too bad, but every time we spoke, it was like he kicked the feet right from under me. I couldn't find my steadiness when he was around, and I didn't appreciate it.

I whirled on him as we turned the corner and ended up in a small arboretum. There were plants all around us, and we had entered a small glass enclosure that seemed to be empty other than the ferns and flowers themselves. "I don't know what's wrong with you, but you need to stop acting like a dick every time I'm around."

He just grinned. "Feisty, I'm always a dick. And as you saw it that one time, you know I know how to use it."

I narrowed my eyes. "What the hell is with you? You are such an asshole."

"And you don't understand why I keep saying things to set you off," he muttered.

"And why is that?" I asked, my lips suddenly going dry.

"Maybe it's because I like it when you glare at me. I like it when you growl. It's easier to push you away whenever you get all growly like that."

"What the hell are you talking about?" I asked, suddenly very confused.

"Who are you, Sparrow? Why the hell do you keep doing this to me?" he asked quietly, almost as if talking to himself.

"Do *what* to you? You're the one acting like a jerk. I'm the boss in there, and you have to stop undermining my authority. Just because you get off on being an asshole doesn't mean you get to be one to me."

"Oh, now you want to talk about getting off?"

"Stop it," I growled.

"You're right, that was too far. However, I just need to know..."

"Need to know what?" I asked, my voice low.

And then he leaned forward and pressed his lips to mine. I gasped, my mouth parting, and he swiped his tongue against mine. I was possessed. That had to be the reason I wasn't pushing him away. I put my hands on his chest, but I didn't push. Instead, I dug into him, and I let him deepen the kiss. I let him guide me slowly farther into the arboretum, my back to the glass, and I groaned against him as he kissed me harder, his lips mashing against mine. This was insanity; this was wrong.

What the hell was wrong with me? I was letting him kiss me, and I didn't push away.

And when he finally let me breathe, he pressed his forehead to mine and I knew I had just made a terrible mistake.

Chapter 8
BRECK

Royal questions... never royal answers.

WHAT THE HELL WAS THAT?

You know what it was—the best damn kiss you've ever had.

She tasted sweet with a hint of spice. And she made the best sounds I'd ever heard. Like a low purring. I could still feel her lips on mine. Even though she'd torn them away in a rush and backed away from me like I was the monster going to eat her alive.

You very well could eat her alive.

In the infinite moments of that kiss, I wanted to show her just what I'd learned while being a lay-about prince most of my life. I might be useless in my family's eyes, but I knew just how to find all the hidden places on a woman, with my tongue, my fingers, my mouth.

I could teach her how to scream *God yes, right there* in over ten languages. And she would completely own me, and fuck, would I let myself be owned.

My hands itched to dive into her hair and tighten, angling her head just how I liked it to kiss her deeper. Or even better, gripping the softness to keep myself from losing my shit when she used her tongue and luscious lips on me.

It was probably for the best that she marched off, but my hands itched with the need to touch her. And I still didn't even understand why the fuck she was so different. I could have any woman I wanted. If my face or my bank account didn't do it, my title usually did. But my body and my brain were fixated on the one woman who had made it perfectly clear she loathed me.

When Wilder had assigned me babysitting duty, I thought it would only take a few hours, if that. Maybe. But then I couldn't seem to stay away from her. Which was a problem in and of itself. And now that I'd gone and kissed her, I knew there would be no forgetting that. No pretending it never happened. No going back to normal. Because I needed to know more, to have more. Needed to taste her again, to touch her.

I didn't have many choices. I could stand there like an idiot, go back to the office, or I could go home, check my remote setup, find the idiot who tried to hurt her, and do my level best to forget that she just owned a little bit of my soul. The worst part was that it was so damned effortless. So easy for her. I had felt like I was drowning in that kiss, like I was honestly losing everything that had me tethered to this realm. But she'd just backed up and seemed completely unaffected. Fine by me. We could both pretend, couldn't we?

Except, you want more.

Damn, I did want more. Ever since the wedding when she'd walked into one of the guest rooms where I was occupied with a couple of female guests, I hadn't been able to get her out of my mind. She'd been so indignant. So irritated. So annoyed. And of course, I loved every moment of getting her hackles up. She thought she knew me, thought she knew who I was and what I was about. She was wrong though. Good luck telling her that. She'd made up her mind about me on the spot, which was fine. Most people did.

Or you gave them a reason to.

Sparrow Bridges wouldn't be the first woman to misjudge me. She wouldn't be the first one to make her assumptions and dismiss me. But she was the first one in a while that hurt.

But I didn't have to stick around for this.

Instead of going back into the office, I took the coward's way out. Which was, let's face it, the perfect course. I sent her a text.

Breck: *I'm going to check out some things on my system. I'll text you if I find anything.*

I felt like I was waiting a lifetime for her to respond. A lifetime for her to answer, to tell me to come back, it was okay. Just an awkward moment. Or better yet, to come back and finish that kiss.

But neither happened. Nope. Instead, her response was brief.

Sparrow: *Okay.*

I scowled and then forced myself to swallow the disappointment. I was used to this.

Breck: *Have Niko make sure you get home. Text me when you're there.*

Sparrow: *Sure.*

She wasn't a fan. That was fine, because just as soon as we found the idiot who thought he could attack her, I'd be done on my part. Wilder could take over and play the hero. He was good at that.

As I headed back to the palace, I tried to convince myself I was okay with that. Wilder, my younger brother, being the hero. Specifically, Sparrow's hero. Speak of the devil, and he shall appear. My phone rang, and I scowled at it. "What do you want, baby brother?"

"I'm checking in on how things are going with Sparrow."

"Fine. Everything is fine." I tried my best to keep my tone even. I knew my brother was too good at reading people to let it slide, but still, I held on to hope. So much hope.

"What's wrong?"

"Nothing. Like I said, I'll help her. Everything is as it should be."

Wilder gave me a rare chuckle. "Is she driving you crazy yet?"

So he knew. He knew what he had done to me. "So you did this on purpose?"

"No, not exactly on purpose. She does need help, and you happen to have the skills that she needs."

"You know, karma is a bitch. Revenge is an even nastier bitch."

I could practically hear him rolling his eyes. "If you think I orchestrated this just so you'd talk to her, I didn't."

"No, I know you didn't. But let's just say I think you could have easily handled the security aspect of this yourself. You don't need me to work on the systems. They're *your* systems."

"Yes, but I am busy."

"Busy doing what?"

"See, there's your problem, big brother, questioning me. I needed your help, I reached out, and you were available. Quit your bitching."

"Brother, you know this is not my forte."

Wilder's chuckle was low. "What's the problem? She's fun, and spunky, and smart. So smart. What's not to like?"

"I just don't like her. She's a pain in the ass."

Liar. You like her plenty.

Wilder laughed again. "Okay, maybe you dig that."

"What? Please, I need ease in my life. I've had enough trouble lately. I'd prefer an old delicate-looking flower."

My brother sighed. "Honestly, give her a chance. I think you two could actually work well together."

"Are you joking? This is me you're talking to. For all the jokes about your name, I'm the wild one. I don't think there's anything wild about her."

"Maybe not. But maybe that's what she needs."

"Is there a purpose to this call?"

"Yes. I wanted to find out how it's going. And then I wanted to ask you to convince her to come and stay at the palace. I'd be more comfortable if she were under our roof."

I laughed at that. "Have you ever tried to convince this woman to do anything she doesn't feel like doing?"

My brother cursed under his breath. "I have already tried to convince her myself, actually. It didn't go well. That's why I thought you might have better luck."

"Hardly. She's not exactly into me telling her what to do."

"Come on, Breck, you can be convincing."

"Again, you're talking to the wrong brother. Ask Roman. He can convince anyone to do anything, which serves him well as king."

There was another beat of silence, and when Wilder spoke again, his voice was soft. "You know, I don't think you give yourself nearly enough credit. You can joke and mock all you want, but I know you. I know that, deep down, you are not the black-hearted playboy. You care. I called, and you came, no questions asked. You said what you needed. You're smarter than you give yourself credit for. I think you're not quite the fuck-up you think you are."

I chuckled uncomfortably at that. Ever since we were kids, I'd always been trying to prove myself to Roman, to Wilder. Hell, even to London. London was the youngest when our parents died. Roman's place was set, and in many ways, so was Wilder's, because he was quieter and younger and didn't face the same pressure I did as 'the spare.' But I wasn't settled; I needed my parents, but they were gone. There was a part of me that was forever trying to prove that I was deserving of who I was.

"Look, I understand the tension between you and Sparrow. I get it. Just be careful, because she's not that girl you think you know. I am telling you this because I think you guys would work well together. I think the two of you would make a good team. That's why. No other reason. I know you're hell on women, but that's because you don't see yourself clearly enough. I think you probably need to cut yourself a little slack."

"I don't need any slack."

"If you say so. But either way, you're the best man for this job."

"You keep saying those words, *best man* and *job*. This is just a favor, and that's it. A favor for our new brother. I like Kannon a lot, and it seems that I should keep his employee from getting herself killed."

My brother sighed. "Okay, if you insist on looking at it that way, then keep her from getting killed. Yes, please. I'm sure Kannon would very much like her in one piece. Also, do it for London, because she's become very close to our sister. And for me. I quite like Sparrow."

I didn't know why, but that last bit set my teeth on

edge. I'd seen the two of them always whispering and laughing. Thick as thieves. Wilder insisted he saw her as family. But was that true? Sometimes I caught him looking at her, and I couldn't understand the edge of jealousy that rode me when it came to my brother. I had no difficulty with women. None whatsoever. I loved them. They loved me.

I'd never had to fight my brothers for a woman, except throne chasers who made it clear they'd be willing to bed all three of us if it increased their chances of wearing a tiara. And really, who wouldn't want one of those?

But the relationship between Sparrow and Wilder irked me, and I wasn't sure why I was so mad about it. I just was. The way he'd parked himself in that chair overnight in the infirmary, watching her sleep. The way he'd sat sentry. I'd wanted to sit sentry. But Wilder was my brother, and I loved him, so I wasn't going to fight him over a girl. I was just going to have to get past this. It was one kiss. Hardly the end of the world. I'd just do what he said and keep her at arm's length. "You can count on me. I'm not going to mess her up. She's not my type anyway."

"I'm not saying you would mess her up, because I don't think you would. She deserves someone serious, someone who's willing to settle down. That's not you yet. If it was, I think you would be perfect for her."

I grumbled at that. "I'm not perfect for anybody. Are we done here?"

"Yes. Fine. We're done. Any luck on finding out who's after her?"

I sighed. "The bugger was smart. He kept his face turned away from the public cameras, so I'm going to businesses and private residences. There are a lot of home security systems in the area. Tracking him should be a little easier. We'll get him."

"I know you will."

We finished the call and hung up, and I had to admit Wilder was right. I had no business going anywhere near Sparrow once her attacker was found. The only problem was, now that I had tasted her, I wasn't sure I could stay away.

Chapter 9
SPARROW

Royal uneasiness wears the crown.

I NEEDED to get my head in the game and not focus on what the hell happened with Breck. He must have done something to me, hypnotized me with his eyes. Or his voice. It must have been the voice. Because there was no way I would've let him kiss me like that if I had been in my right mind. Of course hypnosis was the only answer.

Are you sure about that?

I grumbled at myself as I pressed my fingers to my still-tingling lips. Maybe I'd hit my head harder during the attack than anyone knew about and gotten some sort of slow-onset concussion or something.

Or you wanted *him to kiss you.*

I pinched the bridge of my nose and told myself I just needed a minute. If I could get over whatever the hell had just happened, I would be fine.

But I didn't feel fine. I felt like I was tumbling down into an abyss I wasn't ready for. And that was enough of that. I didn't have time to wallow or worry about my feelings or what the hell had just happened. I didn't have time to remember the taste of Breck's lips. Or the sounds that he made, or his rock-hard body pressed against mine. Because that was never going to happen again. It had just been a foolish mistake, and I didn't need to focus on him.

I needed to focus on my job, the men that reported to me, and keeping them safe. Then I needed to worry about my assignments and make sure when Kannon came back, it was as if he hadn't been gone at all.

That was my job, not worrying about Prince Breck and that stupid mouth of his. I had ninety-nine problems, and the prince wasn't one of them.

My phone buzzed, and I looked down at it, expecting it to be Niko asking me where I was. It was my best friend Onyx. We had a standing Sunday date, and since she had recently moved to the UK and was settling in with my adorable godson, we usually kept to our timetable. Frowning, I quickly answered. "Onyx?

Are you okay?" I asked, my heart rate ticking up as I anticipated a problem. I was well aware of why she had to move to London, so I prayed nothing was wrong.

Or maybe you're on edge.

Okay, fine. I was a little on edge. I'd just go ahead and chalk that up to stress. And it had nothing to do with Breck.

Liar.

"I'm fine. No need to sound so worried. You missed our call last week, so I figured I'd call to see how you were settling into Princesslandia. A far cry from our stomping grounds in Silver Spring."

I let out a breath and relaxed, leaning against the wall. Onyx and I had grown up together in the DC Beltway. Our inauspicious meeting had taken place in AP physics when she'd turned around to ask me if I had any clue what was happening on the chalkboard.

"You have any idea what he's talking about?"

"No clue. I'm screwed."

"Me too. I'm Onyx by the way."

We'd been tight ever since. She'd emotionally patched me up after my disastrous affair with my supervisor... The one who had neglected to mention he already had a fiancée when he took me ring shopping. And I'd been the one to help her forcibly extricate from her ex-husband. Kannon and the whole team had helped with that one. He was the reason she was now in London.

"A very long way. For both of us. How is London treating you?"

"Good. Eli is adjusting to nursery school, and work is going well, but tell me about you. Last time I monopolized the conversation as I bemoaned these tiny European refrigerators. Has the new office opened yet? Were you able to escape to see your parents in Mauritius before you had to play big badass boss lady?"

I laughed at that. "I hardly feel like a boss lady. Mostly I'm trying not to shit the bed. There's a lot riding on this, and I need to get it right."

"Always so hard on yourself. Where is my ass kicker of a bestie?"

"She's right here and always harder on herself than anyone else would be. Failing isn't an option I allow myself." I sighed, trying to stay positive. "It's fine. It's going to be great. And as for Mauritius, everything happened so quickly. So I'll need to wait until Jasmine's wedding."

My little sister was tying the knot, and my mother was in full-on mother-of-the-bride mode. Jasmine though, true to her sweet nature, was the least bridezilla of brides ever.

And her fiancé was lovely... Not that I'd run a background check on him.

Kannon had.

"You're so busy these days. I was worried something was up. You okay?"

There was a pause, and I was afraid I had said too much, but then Onyx cleared her throat. "Nothing's wrong. I just wanted to see how you were doing. I saw the photos that you sent."

"Did you show Eli?" I asked, speaking of my godson. He hadn't wanted to move to London when Onyx had gotten her job offer. Luckily, it had been a great transition for him once he'd discovered he was good at soccer, or football as his friends called it.

I could hear the smile in her voice as she answered. "I did. For some reason, he was waiting for you to send a picture of you in a little tiara or maybe a pretty floofy dress."

I snorted and then just let myself laugh out loud. "Really? He knows I'm going to be the person in a suit protecting that princess, not the actual princess herself, right?"

Though I'd had my mouth on a prince just a few moments ago, but I wasn't going to think about that. Nor was I going to tell my best friend. I loved Onyx, but I wasn't one for going through all of my emotions with anybody, let alone over a phone where anyone could overhear me. Besides, I needed to process first. Once I had processed exactly what I was feeling, then...

No, nobody needed to know what I had just done with Breck. I needed to just forget it because it would *not* be happening again.

"I don't know. You can probably protect somebody in a dress. You'd be good at it. I can see you with one of those thigh-high slits and a garter holster."

"I had to wear high heels and a dress with a slit up to my thigh once so I could fit in. It sucked."

"I bet you looked hot though," she said.

"Of course, I did. But the guys got to wear tuxes, and I didn't. And when I threatened all of them if they dared to look at an inch of my skin, they were quick not to comment."

"You know they don't make fun of you unless it's the normal razzing that they all give each other."

"True, I'm very grateful that they're not all legitimate macho men. Just slightly macho men."

"You're just as macho. It's that whole protective instinct. You get all growly, and I bet you the ladies swoon too."

"Maybe," I said on a laugh.

"It's good to hear your voice, babes." There was something in Onyx's voice that worried me.

"It's good to hear your voice too. I miss you. I hate that I don't see you as much anymore. But enough about me, how are you?"

She sighed. "Well, it was bound to happen. You're over there taking over the world. I love Kannon, and I'm really glad that he's happy and married. I did resent him a little for taking you away from me when you started working for him, but you've had some adventure too."

I cringed, knowing that it was true, even though I hated it. "I wasn't *always* traveling around the world."

"No, sometimes you were in New York, or Michigan. Yes, that was a weird trip with you in Michigan."

"There's nothing wrong with Michigan," I laughed.

"No, there isn't. But I do miss when you were able to visit more. And Eli does too. Come to London. We'll do Jack the Ripper tours and eat too many scones."

"Just twist the knife a little harder," I complained.

"Sorry! I didn't mean to. I called to see how you were doing, not have a little pity party of my own."

"You know, you're always welcome to visit here. I'd love to see the two of you."

"Maybe. But with my job and school and every-thing, it gets a little complicated."

As were the other things that were left unsaid. It seemed we both were doing our best not to talk about important things in our lives. I mean, it's not like she knew what I was ignoring. And once again, I needed to push that from my mind because I didn't have time to think about it.

"Anyway, I miss your face. I love you and be safe."

"All of that right back at you," I said, sighing. "I wish you were here."

"You know what? Staying in a castle, on a royal island, with hot princes all around? I kind of wish I was there too."

"The princes may be hot, but they're a little grumbly." Wilder wasn't too pleased with me. And well, Breck was just your garden variety pain in the ass.

Onyx snorted. "Oh? What about the king? Is he all grumbly?"

"I take it you've seen photos of King Roman?"

"You can't see me, but I'm fanning myself right now. Those Waterford brothers are sexy as hell."

"And a couple of them don't make me want to scream." I bit my lip, annoyed I had said anything.

There was a muffled voice in the distance. "Damn it, I need to go, but next time we talk, we're going to dissect exactly what you meant right there. I need to know which prince is making you scream, because, hell yes."

"I meant in frustration," I growled.

"Sure you did, Sparrow. I totally believe you."

"I love you, jerk," I said, laughing.

"And I love you too. Have fun screaming."

She hung up, and I shook my head, a smile planting on my lips. Hearing her voice was exactly what I needed. I might not have told her everything that I needed to get off my chest, but I was at least a little calmer. I let out a breath and made my way back to Breck's office.

Jaye was still there, going over files, but the prince was gone.

"Sorry it took me a while."

Olly and Niko both gave me a weird look, staring at my face, and I could have kicked myself for not checking my reflection in the mirror to see if my Chapstick was smudged or not.

Niko cleared his voice and said, "No problem. Breck texted and said he'd get on his part of the job soon. He had another meeting, but Jaye's staying."

"Yes, I am," Jaye said, waving before going back to work.

"Anyway, Breck already has a few things done for us, which I have to say, is far more than I expected," Olly grumbled remotely.

My head shot up at the same time as Jaye's.

"What do you mean?" I asked.

"Oh, you guys haven't seen him work?" Jaye asked, confusion on her face before she blinked it away.

"What should I be seeing? What the hell does Breck do?"

Jaye's face went carefully blank. "He does what he always does. I should get back to my desk. I have a lot of things to do. But we will help. Thank you so much for that info though, Olly. It was great to meet you. Even digitally."

Olly met her gaze, blushing. "Well, you know, being digital is still meeting people. Not everything has to be in person."

Was Olly... *flirting?* We all froze before Jaye said goodbye and practically ran out of the room.

I blinked at Olly. "You know, I'm pretty sure you just offered to have cybersex with Breck's assistant."

"I did not," Olly spluttered, and I snorted.

Niko shook his head. "I'm pretty sure that's sort of what you said. I mean, we knew you had no game, but that's a little ridiculous."

"I have game. And I wasn't trying to hit on Jaye. She was nice. And really smart. And shut up."

I met Niko's gaze, and we both burst out laughing.

"You know, I'm going to be living on that same island with you. I will get you back for this," Olly warned.

"What are you going to do?" I asked. "Splutter at me some more?"

"Okay, boss, you're mean. You're letting your power go to your head."

"Well, I'm not your boss, and I guess I just have to make fun of you for the both of us," Niko said. Olly rolled his eyes before we got back to work.

"Okay, other than that little incident here, which we're working on, we have four assignments coming up," I reminded them.

Olly nodded. "We've got it. The two of you are going to be in Alden for a while setting up, and I'm going to be here training my replacement, but the rest of our team is going to be out on assignment."

"And Kannon is going to be checking in every hour like he has been since he went on his trip with London."

Niko sighed. "This is supposed to be his vacation," he mumbled. "Well, at least as much a vacation as you can get when you're still protecting the princess of Alden."

"When is the last time our boss actually took a vacation?" I drawled.

"How about the beginning of never?" Olly asked.

"Exactly."

"Of course, you're just as bad," Niko said as he looked at me.

"Excuse me? You are even worse."

Niko shrugged. "It's the job. Who needs a social life or outside connections when you have our team?"

I remembered Breck's mouth on mine and exactly what I'd wanted him to do to me just outside this room, and I dutifully ignored that comment.

Because I didn't need anything more than I already had. I had enough on my plate as it was. And I sure as hell didn't need Prince Breck and that very talented mouth of his. Even though, as I got to know him better, I realized he might not exactly be the fuck-up that I imagined him to be at first.

Just who exactly was he? And why couldn't I put him out of my mind?

Chapter 10
SPARROW

It's never who you expect.

AS IT TURNED OUT, Breck wasn't at all bad.

You mean you're starting to like him?

No, I didn't say that. But in the week since we'd kissed, he'd been kind. Nice even. Available. Hopeful. I was actually starting to wonder about the amount of time he was spending on tracking the relays and possible routes my attacker had taken. Originally, it was supposed to be only a couple of days to appease Wilder. I didn't expect anything to come out of it, really. I mean, it was only a mugging, right?

I dropped my groceries at the back of my car. I hated

the fact that because of one stupid incident, everything about my movements had changed. Where once I'd felt so capable, able to take care of myself in any situation, now I needed to be more careful and aware.

Because you were not careful and not aware that time. Remember when you got jumped?

I sighed, locking the trunk of my car and smiling at the little girl selling flowers in front of the market. She and her mother had been there every Saturday so far since I'd been in Alden, and I always said I was going to buy some when I fully settled into my flat. Maybe flowers would cheer me up. I left the parking area for the grocery store and smiled as I approached her. The crowds were thicker, but that was safer, wasn't it? The sun was high and everything about the surroundings screamed old-world Europe. Like time had wound backward and the streets were lined with cobblestones where the villagers made their fortunes on whatever they sold at their stalls.

I greeted her and she smiled back. "Which flowers would you like?"

"I don't know, maybe these. I do like the red and purple."

She gave me a sage nod, as if saying, yes, those were exactly the flowers I needed to have in my home for that bright, fun, lived-in feeling.

She added some baby's breath and some other little green sprigs I couldn't identify. As I watched her roll them up, I inhaled deeply the mixture of scents, flowers and vegetables and something delicious. Onion, ginger, and garlic cooking somewhere. Someone must be selling some kind of meat in a stall because, God, my stomach grumbled, and I wanted to follow the smell.

"What's your name?"

"Clara."

"Well Clara, I've never seen anyone make such a pretty bunch of flowers as you have."

"Well, you should see my mother. She makes the best bouquets. She's just so good at it."

I smiled at the woman who was unloading a tray of flowers from the back of a van, and she gave me a smile and a head nod. I waved at her. "I don't know, Clara, it might take a lot of convincing to prove to me that she's better than you are."

Clara grinned at me then. I paid her and then headed to see if I could find the source of the delicious smell. I'd made the age-old mistake of going grocery shopping when I was hungry.

Not wise, I know. Rookie mistake. But I had been wise in my shopping list. Besides, I wanted to spend more time in Oldtown. Most tourists stuck to the glitzier side of Alden, but the locals came here. There were a few tourist attractions on this side of the island, but this was where locals bought their food, not the fancy grocery store I'd just been tromping around in. This was where negotiations happened, barters, quick trade. I couldn't help but smile. When I finally found the stall the delicious smells were wafting from, I groaned when I saw the line already six people deep. I could go back to my car, or I could wait it out.

My stomach grumbled, telling me its choice. I knew that was the better move anyway, because it wasn't like I had time to cook. Getting the office ready to open, we'd had potential clients come in, so there had been meetings. And obviously, Breck had been up my ass as well.

My libido stretched inside as if the idea of Breck anywhere near my ass was a possibility.

Stand down. He's not here.

She went back to sleep, and I shifted on my feet. There was a crackling in the air that I couldn't quite place or explain. I was restless. The line shifted and I sighed with relief. Okay, so it was some kind of salami sandwich? I didn't care, because right now, it sounded like bloody heaven.

"Come with me quickly, and no one gets hurt."

There was something pressing into my back. Gun?

I held myself perfectly still, trying to assess the situation. How had I not noticed someone had come up behind me? How had I missed the weapon? If I fought my way out of this right now, would anyone else get hurt?

"I'm sure you don't want to do this. I'm quite a handful. I promise. Just be on your way, and I won't have to hurt you."

He leaned close, and I could smell his sour breath. Like day-old ale. "Shut up, you bitch, and move."

Clara ran up with a bunch of flowers for a woman in line three places ahead of me, and I knew he had me. I didn't want anyone else to get hurt just because I knew I could fight my way out of this situation.

With a sigh, I nodded. "Okay, you can relax. I'm not going to do anything stupid."

"I've heard that before."

He led me back the way I'd come, but the crowds had gotten thicker now. When we made a left by one of the clothing stalls into a darker alley, a woman with her bundles bumped us, and I seized my opportunity. I shoved my hips back into his, moving him back a step and creating space between our bodies. After that I shoved my hand back into his groin, making sure to make hard contact with the heel of my hand. And then I ran. Through the crowds, I zoomed in and out, careful to avoid bumping into anyone. I took a left and then a sharp right and ran down the long hallways of tucked-in stores. Stores that had been built into the walls. I ran toward the palace, toward the office, away from my car. Never mind that I had ice cream melting in my trunk. I didn't care. I knew safety was this way and less likelihood of anyone else getting hurt.

I made a sharp left, but I'd made a gross miscalculation. *Dead fucking end.*

I whirled around, intending to run in the opposite direction, but there were two men already in the alleyway. Both enormous. Bigger than Kannon. Six feet four inches. Sculpted. One had a jagged scar down his face, and they both had beady little eyes. "What are the chances you're going to let me walk away from this?"

The uglier of the two, arguably, snarled at me. "Shut up, bitch."

"Oh, aren't you loquacious? Fantastic." The other one smiled at me. A genuine smile. "Look, you don't want to hurt me, right?"

He shrugged. "On the contrary, I do want to hurt you. I'd like to hurt you very much."

"Oh, you have weird hobbies, you know that?"

He chuckled and shrugged, flexing his hands before curling them into fists.

"Ugh, really? It's so déclassé to hit a woman. Or don't you know that?"

The other one stepped forward. "Not when she's a bitch like you."

"Okay, so we're doing this?"

I didn't have much room. The alley was tight. But I had one advantage. Speed. I was faster. I just couldn't get hit.

Big and less ugly ran for me, aiming to knock me on my back. But I spun and plastered myself against the wall. And as he sailed by, I released an elbow as I spun around to face the uglier of the two and hit him straight in the kidney. He cursed as he stumbled forward.

I didn't have much time. I used the small element of surprise and leverage to run for ugly.

He expected me to go low, but no, I lunged my whole body at him, attaching myself to him, spider-monkey style. Gripping my hands on either side of his face, I used my thumbs to press into his eye sockets and pushed. He yowled as he clawed at me.

While he was fighting, I used my head. And even though I knew better, I headbutted him. Headbutts were the worst. You ran the risk of concussing yourself in the process, but it was a weapon I had in a land of no weapons.

He clawed at me as he tried to wrap his hands around me. I swung my legs, managing to land a decent strike to the side of his knee, which made him drop and gave me better leverage. I pulled him down. With my hands already on his cheeks, I adjusted my grip to his ears, and pulled his head down, leveraging my weight backwards slightly so I could deliver a knee directly to his face. I shoved his body aside and took off running, desperate to clear his feet, but he scissored his legs, tripping me. I knew the fall was imminent, and I knew those cobblestones were going to hurt. There was no room for a tuck and roll, so I landed the only way I could. Forearms pressed out like I was going to do a half plank, and I whipped my head to the side to avoid smashing my face into the stone.

But there was no rest for the wicked. I managed to land on my forearms for safety instead of putting my arms straight out. They still stung and burned from the impact though. My breath whooshed out of my lungs, and I was too stunned to drag in another.

With a groan, I turned on my back, cognizant of keeping my hands up to protect my face in case a blow came toward me. As another deterrent, I put up a foot, but the first guy I'd taken down was big and nasty, and he grabbed hold of my foot. He dragged me and I screamed. Aiming for his chin with my other foot, I only made it to his knee, but I got a good enough angle to hurt him a little, and he temporarily dropped me.

When he released me, I pushed myself to my feet

and bolted. One foot in front of the other, I ran blindly and narrowly escaped the alley, but I knew they were on my tail. I shoved my way through the crowd, less careful now. I had no room for politeness. This was about survival.

I ran and dashed, and ran and dashed. Finally, I ran toward a long gateway which widened into a road, and I was sprinting by the time I got there. *Four hundred meters.* I could make it. I was fast. I ran track in high school.

Three hundred meters. I could hear the footsteps behind me, giving chase.

There were some people milling around, but they were mostly walking dogs in the opposite direction, because this way was toward the palace really, but the offices and most businesses that line the street were closed because it was fucking Saturday.

Unless you had business in the palace, you wouldn't go this way. You would go the other way to the main entrance. God, I'd made the worst choice ever. There would be no random passersby going this way.

I glanced around frantically. Maybe I could make it to my flat. It was entirely possible.

Two hundred meters.

The feet behind me were stomping faster, harder, closer.

And then out of the blue, from the right, from somewhere I hadn't even expected, I was rushed, tackled from the side, and my whole world froze for an instant. For the first time in my life, I understood what 'hang time' meant. Those brief seconds between movement and impact, when you really could imagine and feel every moment of your life.

And then I hit the ground, cold stone rattling my bones. Unable to protect myself in a better falling position, my shoulder groaned in agony. And worse, I couldn't fucking breathe because some idiot was on top of me.

Even though I was injured, I wasn't down for the count.

I tried to remember everything I'd ever been taught. From wrestling with my dad and my cousins, to all my self-defense classes, the number one rule was never let a man get on top of you. Never. Not once. And so I scooted out from under him and instinctively began the movements I'd learned in jiu-jitsu and Krav Maga, wriggling my body like a shrimp from side to side like I was doing crunches for my obliques. And every time I came into my crunch, I hit him with whatever blow I could manage. Unfortunately, those blows were one-armed. My shoulder hurt too much. I couldn't even move that arm.

"You bitch."

I didn't waste any breath on him, but I thought, *What, you can't be more original?*

My own sarcasm gave me the extra oomph I needed when he grabbed for me again. Unlucky for him, I drew my foot back and landed a straight heel kick to his face. Blood splattered everywhere.

I scrambled to my feet once again and tried to distance myself from both my assailants, but I saw there was another man running down the street.

Shit. What the hell?

I was having one hell of a terrible day. And then, after this was over, I was going to have ice cream to clean up.

That is if you survive.

Fuck that. I was going to survive. Today was a really shitty day to die.

The man with the scar was not willing to play this time. He threw a punch, and I only narrowly ducked it as I tried to run past him. I threw an elbow, only to have it blocked. He caught my wrist then spun me around and tried to trap me in a bear hug.

My good arm was locked, so I had to use the bad one. I screamed in agony as I twisted it just so, then I grabbed his dick, squeezed, and turned my wrist.

Through a wheeze, he cursed me. "Fuck you."

"Not today, you asshole."

With just enough space between us, I delivered my elbow backward, but it didn't really do much. Nevertheless, it did free my other arm some. As he created space, I delivered another elbow back toward his face and then turned my body and stuck my thumb in his eye socket. Again, he yowled, releasing me. When I tried to run past him again, he grabbed me with one arm, and then his other arm backhanded me.

As I thought about how I was going to die, of all the ways to go, all I could think was *Hey, I got my ass kicked in the fight, but the one move I never thought would down me was a backhand.* That was such a bitch move.

Bitch slapped.

Hardy-har.

My subconscious was in one hell of a hilarious mood today.

Still, the pain shattered along my cheek, my jaw, and my head exploded in agony. I was stunned. Too stunned to do anything good and useful.

Until he clamped his hand around my throat and lifted me off the ground.

I kicked wildly, even though I knew that was the wrong move. I was wasting valuable energy. I tried to raise both my arms above my head, but my one arm would not cooperate. All I had to do was raise them up and bring them back down. But I only managed the move with one arm, and it was ineffective. My air supply was going, and the pain and dizziness started to take over. The shades of gray on the edges of my vision were closing in fast. And then my assailant leaned forward. "Truman says hi. You never should have gone after him, bitch."

I frowned. "Truman?"

Suddenly, my blood ran cold. The case from two years ago. We'd spirited away the wife of a Hollywood exec. The vilest sort of man. Raped his wife repeatedly. Abused her. She'd finally gotten the courage to leave and needed a safe way to do it. When she told her story, we discovered he was an all-around asshole and not just to his wife. Five other women came forward, and he was charged with multiple counts of rape and assault. He'd gone to jail. And fucking Christ, this was his retaliation.

But then, suddenly, I was released. The air that had seemed like a luxury not five seconds earlier was suddenly plentiful again. Something was happening. Noise. I tried to drag my eyes open, but all I saw was the third man. The one I'd worried about that had been meters away when I had engaged with Scarface. He was doing something to Scarface, making him gurgle. All I saw was a series of kicks, punches, blocks, spinning kicks, a brutal fight. And then Scarface went down, slumping onto the cobblestones. Then there were other people there. Several people. Oh God. My head felt like it was going to pop off my neck.

Somewhere in the distance, as the gray came back into my field of vision, wanting to take over, wanting to pull me down so I didn't have to think about the pain in my head, I could have sworn I heard Breck's voice. "Jesus fucking Christ, Sparrow? Sparrow, are you okay?"

And even though I was certainly not okay, I felt a whole hell of a lot better knowing that Breck was holding me. But I knew that had to be a dream of my delusional, about-to-die mind because there was no way Breck was going to wrap his arms around me and make this all okay. It didn't matter how much I wished it.

Chapter 11
BRECK

How many frogs until you find the prince?

"I'D LOVE to know why you keep looking at me like that."

I barely resisted the urge to snarl at Sparrow. Instead, I took a deep breath and glared. "You're getting another black eye, and they just had to check to see if you had another concussion. Don't tell me you're fine," I snapped.

It had been a few hours since the attack, and I knew there would be questions and inquiries and everything else that needed to be done in order to see what the fuck had just happened, but all I could do was focus on the newly formed bruises near Sparrow's eye.

We were in the infirmary, waiting to see when we could leave, and though the doctor had already seen her, I could barely control my temper. Me. The guy who never blew up. I usually acted out... in other ways. And yet, every time I was around Sparrow, I couldn't help it. She did things to me I didn't like.

Oh, pretty sure you do like them.

Sparrow stared at me, and I shrugged. "I didn't have a concussion the last time, therefore, I can't have *another* concussion if I didn't have the first one. And, as you heard, the doctor just left after saying I don't have a concussion. I'm fine. And I have work to do, so if you could just get out of my way, I can get it done."

"You're not working tonight," I growled.

She let out a breath, her shoulders tightening ever so slightly. She masked the movement before I could comment on it. She was so good at hiding her emotions from everyone and yet... Sometimes I felt like I could see beneath the surface.

"And we've already discussed the fact that you're not my prince, not my king, and not my boss."

"And your boss isn't here," I growled.

Her eyes narrowed slightly. "No, he's not. That means I'm in charge here. And now that I've passed my evaluation, I need to get back to work. I have a job to do, Breck."

"Really?" I raised my chin in disbelief. "Because you were clinging to me out there, and it scared the hell out of me, Sparrow. I don't know what's going on, but I'm not letting you out of my sight."

She tilted her head again, studying my face, her own expression cool and calm. "I'm sorry, when did we decide you were allowed to tell me what to do?"

"When I thought you were going to die and ran to save you. That's when."

She shook her head, a small smile playing on her lips. "Not even then, Breck. You don't get to be my keeper."

"Well, maybe somebody should. Hell, Sparrow. Those men could've killed you."

"But they didn't. I'm trained. I know what I'm doing." She paused. "I've been doing this a long time, Breck. I can handle myself."

"You can, but you should still rest for the night," Niko said, barreling past me into the room. I glared at the other man, but he ignored me. "We're on it tonight, you get some rest."

Sparrow's shoulders once again tensed, but she relaxed them quickly, looking like the icy, unruffled woman I had come to know... and wanted to know more.

"You too? You're going to play the big, bad dude card right now? If I was a man, would you be telling me to rest?"

Niko snarled, and I was kind of upset that I hadn't been the one to do it first. "Excuse me? Last time I got hurt on the job, and I didn't even require stitches, you made me sit out for a whole day before I was allowed to come back. You need to sit out for at least six hours and try to get some sleep. And then we're going to come back, and we're going to kick someone's ass in the morning. That's all we're asking. You know the rules. You get hurt, and if we're able, you take a break. We need to make sure you're okay."

She looked between us. "I'm fine, and since you added 'if we're able,' *are we?* Kannon's not here. Olly's not here. I'm here. You're here. *We* need to take care of this."

"And nothing is going to get done at this exact moment. So you are going to get rest, and you're going to let Breck here take care of you."

I blinked, shocked, and looked over at Niko. "That's what I was going to say, but I didn't think you'd actually agreed with me."

Niko raised a lip and bared his teeth. He looked like a damn werewolf just then. I was surprised he didn't bare a fang. "We figured somebody is going to need to sit on her and make sure she doesn't have a concussion. Therefore, since it doesn't seem like you have much to do, you're up."

I ignored the tone because I was getting exactly what I wanted. If you could call this what I wanted. "Come on. I'll take care of you, Feisty."

Sparrow shook her head and let out another calming breath. "I don't need anybody protecting me."

"Okay, then I will make sure you have a nice fluffy pillow, and you can get some rest. And then you can take over the world and kick ass tomorrow. Deal?" I asked as Niko and I both glared at Sparrow.

She looked between us, and her shoulders sunk ever so slightly.

I wanted to count that as a win, but I didn't like seeing her so defeated. She was either going to lash out, and Niko and I would end up bloody, or she'd sink into herself, and I'd hate that even more.

Since when had I figured out how she would react so quickly? I knew she intrigued me, but apparently, I had been studying her more than I knew.

"If it will make you both leave me alone for a few hours, then I will take the break. I understand what my duties are, however, and I would appreciate if you'd remember that as well."

"Of course, darling," I sneered. Niko gave me a look,

but I ignored it. I was skating on thin ice, but I needed Sparrow to act normal. I didn't like to see her wounded —not that she had appeared that way for longer than a brief moment.

Sparrow rolled her shoulders back, winced, and I nearly growled. She gathered her things calmly then made her way toward the door, looking as if she hadn't been hurt less than an hour before.

"Coming, prince? I'm pretty sure you need to lead the way."

"I've been waiting forever for you to say those exact words. Come on now, Feisty, let me show you my lair."

"Dear God," Niko muttered under his breath, but I ignored the man.

I was getting what I wanted, even if I hadn't realized this was what I needed.

WE MADE our way to my wing in silence, and I took the back way so there were fewer people to accidentally bump into. Roman was out of the castle for the evening at a function, though he had been made aware of what had happened. And I knew Wilder was working on a thousand different things at once and that I should probably get to work as well. But right then, there was nowhere else I needed to be. Not really. I needed to make sure Sparrow was okay, and I didn't like the fact that it was the first thing I thought of.

Why did I feel like I was losing my mind?

"Well, here it is," I said, entering my first set of rooms.

Her eyes widened, and as she looked at the place, I knew she was studying every inch of it. We were in the formal sitting room, where I did most of my entertaining, though not the same entertaining she was probably thinking of. I had meetings here, and this was where I brought my family. I had one more sitting room, but that one had become my home office, and it was mostly for my use, though Jaye and some of my other staff members came in if we needed extra time and wanted to be a little more comfortable. Nothing playboy happened there.

I had two guest rooms, though I didn't use them because the only people I needed for guests were family. Some of my staff members had slept there before, especially if we had an ice storm or just a late night of working and nobody wanted to drive home.

And then there was my bedroom. My oasis.

Sparrow looked around and cleared her throat.

"I imagined black silk," she said, studying my sizable antique king-size bed.

Like everything in the castle, each piece of furniture

was either made for this generation, or had been passed down from previous ones. I wasn't a huge fan of decorating, so I let the decorators just do what they wanted, although Aunt Rebecca hadn't had any influence over my rooms like she had with London. Everything was all dark blues and creams and was very comfortable.

At least I thought so.

"Well, I didn't feel like going full-on sex tape," I said on a laugh.

"What do the ladies think when you bring them here? Do they expect silk too?"

I gave her a funny look. "No, love, I don't bring women here. You'd be the first."

Her eyes narrowed. "You're just screwing with me."

I *wish*.

I didn't say that out loud. "No, nobody needs to be here but me."

"I've walked in on you and two women before. Please don't tell me you haven't used this bed for something similar."

I held back a wince, still not happy for some reason that she had witnessed that little scene. It hadn't mattered before. I knew she didn't like the person she saw that night, but maybe I wanted her to see the person that no one else did.

And why was I thinking that?

"There are other rooms for things like that; this suite is just for me." I shrugged, then pulled off my suit jacket. "We can get you set up in one of the guest rooms, and I should have a pair of pajamas that might fit you."

"I thought you didn't bring women here?" she asked.

I snorted. "I don't. However, in the guest rooms, I have random sweats in different sizes, because what else are you supposed to fit in drawers so they don't stay empty? And maybe one day, I'll want to have a guest, and I want them to feel comfortable. I don't know. I just have them. Don't complain."

I moved past her, and she put her hand on my forearm, squeezing. I looked down at her and let out a breath, the warmth of her touch on my arm intoxicating me a little.

"I'm sorry. It just seems I don't know you as well as I thought I did."

I met the green of her eyes and swallowed. "No, you don't."

She searched my face, her mouth parting. "Why? Why are you so different?"

"I'm precisely who I need to be, Sparrow."

I looked down at her lips, and I didn't mean to, but then she did the same to mine, and I found myself leaning forward. My lips brushed against hers, and I couldn't help but remember the taste of her before, and how it matched to now, and how I needed more.

"I shouldn't be doing this," I whispered. She stiffened and moved away. I shifted so I had my arm around her waist, but I didn't squeeze. "Because it could hurt you after the attack. Not because I don't want to."

"Then you don't want your first notch on this bedpost?" she asked icily.

I cursed under my breath. "No, I don't know. Shit. You'd think I'd be better at this."

"I thought you were." she said, her gaze searching my face.

"Sparrow," I whispered, my voice trailing off.

"I just... I just need this. You and me. No promises. Just tonight."

I cursed again. "I don't want you to hate me in the morning."

Her lips quirked in a smile. "I thought it was evident that we already hate each other now."

That got a growl out of me, and then I lowered my head again and took her mouth with mine. She moaned into me, wrapping her arms around my waist, kissing me hard.

"I'm going to have to be gentle, so I don't hurt you," I whispered.

"And to think I heard that you liked it a little more than gentle."

I growled against her lips. Then I reached around her and picked her up. She was all muscle and strength, and she leaped into my arms and wrapped her legs around my waist.

"Sparrow," I whispered against her lips.

"Come on, prince, fuck me."

I grinned, loving *this* Sparrow, the one without the ice but all the heat. Then I walked her to the bed, knowing that we shouldn't be doing this. It was probably a fever dream, and I'd wake up in the morning and realize that I had gone to sleep thinking about her. I'd probably end up aching in the morning and regretting everything, but I didn't really care right then.

I sat her on the edge of the bed, touched her face, and kissed her gently.

"I don't want to hurt you."

She studied my face again and swallowed hard. "The bruises are just on my face, so just kiss my lips, and maybe other places."

I hadn't meant physically when I said I didn't want to hurt her, but we were both being cautious about what we *weren't* saying.

I nodded and then brushed a kiss against her lips, and then her jaw, and then her neck. She pulled at my shirt, untucking it from my pants, and then moved so she could undo my belt. I pulled her shirt over her head, careful of any injuries she may have, and cursed when I saw the slight bruises forming on her honey-brown skin.

"Ignore them. I'm tougher than I look."

"I know you're damn tough, Sparrow. Doesn't make me any less angry that someone dared put their hands on you."

"I thought you were here to put your hands on me now," she teased.

"Fine, that I can do."

I lowered my head and latched my mouth onto her nipple over the lace of her bra. She moaned, arching into me, and I kissed between her breasts, before working her bra completely off. Her breasts fell heavy into my hands, and I cupped the sweet mounds, her flesh nearly over-filling my palms.

"Beautiful," I whispered.

"I need to see you."

I grinned and then lapped at first one nipple, then the other. She squirmed on the bed, her legs tightening around me, and I moved away before undoing my shirt. With each flick of a button, her gaze went to my hands, then down to my pants, where my cock pressed against my zipper.

"Soon," I promised.

She growled then reached for me, undoing my zipper and sliding her hand underneath the waistband of my boxer briefs. I groaned when she gripped me and pulled me out of my pants.

"Jesus," I muttered.

"Damn," she said as her hands wrapped around me. And then she lowered her head and flicked the tip of my dick with her tongue.

"God, Sparrow."

"You're taking too long," she muttered, and then swallowed the tip of me. I groaned, slightly pushing into her mouth more with the thrust of my hips. She hummed along me, playing with my balls and the base of my dick as she slowly worked on me. I undid the rest of my shirt and then pulled away, ignoring her moan of protest. Then I tore the rest of my clothes off before going down to my knees. She raised a single sexy brow, and I tugged on her pants, undoing the button, and then her zipper.

"My turn," I muttered.

"Well, if a prince desires." She lifted her ass up off the bed, and I pulled off her pants and panties with one quick movement. They got caught at her boots, and we both looked at each other, snorted, and I worked her boots off quickly. "I thought you were smoother than this, playboy prince."

I growled. "There are so many fucking laces," I muttered. And finally, I had her completely naked in front of me.

She laughed at me again and opened her mouth, probably to say something sarcastic, so I took her thighs in hand, spread her, and licked her folds. She nearly shot off the bed into my mouth and groaned my name.

"That's better," I mumbled, and then went after her clit, sucking and licking and eating every sweet inch of her pussy.

"Breck," she panted. She tugged on my hair, pressed me closer to her heat, and I hummed against her before spearing her with two fingers. She clamped around them and came, her whole body shaking.

I lapped at her before I stood up, cock in hand, and went for a condom.

"Where are you going?" she asked, her hands on her breasts as she lay back against the bed.

"Making sure you're protected since it's my turn."

Her gaze went straight to my cock, and I watched her lick her lips as I slid the condom over my length. I was back on her in a flash, positioning us both in the center of the bed.

"I told you I'd be gentle," I whispered against her, and she reached up and traced her finger along my brow.

"You're not hurting me," she murmured.

"Good," I said, and then I positioned myself at her entrance before I slowly entered her inch by inch.

She groaned, her inner muscles tightening around me as I parted her flesh and stretched her. "Breck."

"Almost there, love," I muttered. And then I was fully seated, and both of us sat there, sweat slicked and shaking. She was so tight, so perfect, and I could barely rein it all in. But I knew I needed to. For both of us.

When she wrapped her arms around me and then her legs around my waist, I slowly began to move, both of us arching for one another. I met her gaze as she blinked at me, and I swore I saw something there. And yet the emotion was so fleeting, I could barely catch it and then she turned away, her eyes closed, but I still felt she was there, meeting me.

I thrust into her, slowly at first, and then faster and harder. Both of us were panting, and I pulled one leg up slightly to go deeper, and she pressed that knee near her shoulder and met my gaze again.

"Finally."

I needed her eyes, that green gaze that never wavered.

Since she had her hand on the back of her thigh, keeping herself spread for me, I slid my hand between us, flicked my thumb over her clit, and she came, her gaze on mine. And I followed her, both of us falling, both of us arching.

I hovered over her as we came back down, and she stared at me, and I knew I saw regret there.

She had fucked the prince she hated.

And now, once again, I would have to deal with the consequences.

Chapter 12
SPARROW

A royal plan... or something.

I COULD FEEL Breck's eyes on me. His gaze slightly narrowed, teeth working over his bottom lip. If I didn't know better, I'd say he was thinking about what happened in his room two nights ago.

Okay, what happened *three times* in his room. But really, who was counting?

You were.

My gaze flickered to his again, and insecurity settled in my gut. He looked mildly irritated. Maybe he was regretting it. What did I know? So, I'd broken my rule and had a one-night stand. With someone I wasn't even sure I liked.

You like him.

I had to admit, even outside of bed, he wasn't *terrible.* Or at least not as bad as I'd thought he was. However, one thing I did know was that he was a playboy. Full-on royal playboy. Sardonic smile, ridiculous bank account, scores of women ready, willing, and able to jump his bones at a moment's notice. And I'd slept with him. Like an idiot.

No sleeping involved really. What with all that shouting, 'Oh, my God, oh, my God.'

Flushing under his gaze, I cleared my throat and turned my attention to the screen. I pressed the button on the remote. "This lovely gentleman here is Truman Nix, big-time Hollywood producer."

Niko rubbed his jaw. "Nix... Nix. Didn't we have a case with him?"

I nodded. "We helped his wife escape her abusive relationship with him. Saturday when I was attacked, one of the idiots in question very clearly said, 'This is for Truman.' So that sent us down a rabbit hole. Come to find out, Nix is out of jail on a technicality. Somebody fucked up the chain of evidence. So he's out and looking for blood."

"Shit," Niko murmured under his breath.

"Nix sent his buddies after me. But I'm not even sure why he did that because I wasn't even that involved in the case. All I did was get his wife to a women's shelter and then help move her into her new digs. It was Kannon's case, but I'm sure he's pissed at all of us."

Niko whistled low as he searched the file. "Wow, he's a piece of work. Lots of rape charges. Why the fuck is he even out?"

I hit the clicker again as I continued to pace. "This is his brother, Matthew Nix, lawyer to the stars. He's a legal shark and is very, very good at his job. He got the LAPD on some evidentiary bullshit."

Breck furrowed his brow. "Does Nix have access to his funds?"

Niko looked up from his screen. "There's no telling how much cash he has stored. He's one of those people that has backup plans on his backup plans. He's a concern because obviously he had some Bitcoin. Do we have eyes on him?"

I shrugged. "Not yet. Supposedly he's laying low at home, but we have zero visual. We can't even spot the guy through a window."

"My guess is he's not there."

Breck frowned. "Have you tried to send in an undercover operative?"

From the video monitor, Olly leaned forward.

"That's a no go. I have tried everything to get onto that property, even girls. Usually hot, lost women will do the trick. Nada. We can't get past security. I have no eyes. I did manage to get a really small drone in there briefly, but then it was spotted and shot down."

Breck frowned. "What's the security company?"

Olly laughed. "Weston Security."

"I'll look into it."

Olly grinned. "Ah yes, while I am bound by certain rules, you are not. So, if you can have a look-see, that would be great. Meanwhile, I need to get back to my case. Do you need me for anything else there? I wish I was on this with you."

"No. I just need whatever information you have since you worked on it before Niko got here."

Niko sat forward rubbing his jaw and sighed. "Okay, if he's out, is he going after his wife?"

Olly shook his head. "She's clean. I literally wiped her off the face of the planet. She is long gone. No trail, no nothing. She took whatever cash she could find, a few million dollars, and opted the simple life. Cash savings, ordinary job, nothing traceable. She's completely off the grid."

Breck nodded at that. "Well, it's the safest plan. How long has she been in hiding?"

I answered that one. "A year and a half. Hell, I don't even know where she is."

Olly spoke up. "Second that. I started the chain and told her that for the first three years, she needed to move once every six months. She's got six passports, so she can go anywhere she needs to go. She should be impossible to find, but if you need me to, I can take a break off of this case and try to locate her."

Breck shook his head. "No, I'll find her."

The center of my chest warmed at the fact that he was so committed to helping. "Breck, unless we can be ultimately discrete, I don't want to disrupt her life. She's been through enough."

His gaze on me was direct, penetrative. "Don't worry, I'll take care of her. I won't leave a footprint."

I nodded. "Thank you."

Niko nodded too. "What do you want me to do?"

"For starters, set up cameras on my place and Kannon and London's new place as well. Fully tricked out. And I want panic rooms installed at both locations as quietly as possible."

Breck laughed. "Niko, you want to talk to Wild for that. He's got great teams. We all have a pied-à-terre outside the palace for those times when we just need to get out. I'd suggest something underground, but that's up to you."

Niko nodded his thanks. "Right, will do."

Marcus chimed in from the video. "If you need me, I can finish up my case in a few days and come out."

I shook my head. "No, that won't be necessary. Besides, you and Olly need to hold down the fort in LA. Olly's going to be needed for his all-time favorite client, and I know you love a starlet."

Olly rolled his eyes. "You don't like me, do you?"

"What was your first hint, me telling you I don't like you? I feel like you owe me. This is your penance."

"So I hacked into your favorite lingerie store one time. I needed a present."

"Inappropriate."

Olly just rolled his eyes. "It's not like you have anything interesting anyway." Breck's gaze narrowed imperceptibly at that. Did he care? Who the hell knew? The man was like a steel trap.

"Where are we on weapons? I still don't have our shipment in."

Niko nodded. "Actually, they arrived at the harbor this morning. I got a call, but we had this meeting. So, once we're done here, I'll go check and make sure we got all the weapons we ordered."

Breck nodded. "You should have said something. I could have sped that up."

"And just how would you have made the ship get here faster?"

He frowned. "I would have done something."

Was he trying to help by flexing his princely muscles?

You like it when he flexes his muscles.

Oh, boy. I did not like the direction my thoughts were taking.

"Okay, Breck, since you and your brother have the two men in custody, how long can we hold them?"

He grinned at me and shrugged his broad shoulders. "Well, indefinitely."

My brows lifted. "What?"

"It's the law. You have the same protection as my future brother-in-law, so the attack was tantamount to treason. It's a stretch for full treason since this wasn't an attack directly on the royal family, but I can hold them indefinitely. They will rot in prison."

"Okay. And if I wasn't getting the royal treatment?"

He shrugged. "In that case, a lawyer would be assigned, and they'd be arraigned within a week. But they'll be sectioned in a separate wing. No bail, obviously, because they are dangerous. They attacked in broad daylight in a very public area and could have hurt citizens of Alden. So, they'll be in a separate wing with no access to visitors. No phone calls in or out. So, if we're going to put together a plan to go after Truman, this is our shot."

"Also, can you talk to Wilder? I want video footage of all ports of entry over the last week."

Breck frowned. "What are you looking for?"

"I'm not sure, but I'll know it if I see it."

"Please, just tell me. I can help you."

I sighed. It wasn't easy sleeping with someone you worked with. But was that even what we were doing? "I'm looking for Nix."

It was Olly that chimed in. "He could be in Alden. And if he's trying to smoke you out, verifying that would be a smart move."

Breck nodded. "I'll have my people start on it. Do you have a recent picture?"

I clicked the remote to back up the slides and put Nix's photo onscreen again then said to him and Niko, "I'll send it over to your tablets too."

Breck nodded. "If he's here, we'll find him."

"Right. Let's just hope he's not here. That adds a complication we don't need."

Niko nodded to me. "Don't worry, Sparrow. We got you."

"I'm not worried about me. I'm worried what happens when London and Kannon get back. Let's see if we can resolve this before that happens. I don't want to add any danger to their lives. I think London's been through enough."

I wasn't sure what that look on Breck's face was about. His expression softened somewhat. And something glimmered in his eyes. It looked an awful lot like respect. But I knew him better than that. Didn't I?

"All right, if Truman Nix is here, let's find him," I said. "Otherwise, let's tighten the borders so that he can't get in, and then let's make sure we fortify the palace walls, as it were, so he doesn't get that close ever again."

Breck's jaw went tight. And he nodded. "He won't. Not on our watch."

AFTER THE MEETING, Niko headed to the harbor to gather our weapons, and Breck lingered. "So, what's the plan for the rest of the afternoon?"

"Well, I have work to do. I've got some case inquiries I need to check out. Contractors I need to talk to. Kannon is very particular about his office space. You know, work stuff."

He frowned at me. "Well, will any of it keep until tomorrow?"

"It's Monday. Besides, what are you getting at?"

He gave me a slight smile as he leaned back against the conference table. He reached out, took my hand, and pulled me to him. "Well, I would like to spend the afternoon with you. I figured I would feed you first and then show you some of Alden."

I opened my mouth to argue, but then I snapped it shut. What the hell were we doing? "I... That's sweet, really. But you don't have to—"

He sighed. "Oh, what? You figure, playboy prince. All-around asshole. Hit it and quit it?"

"Please don't say hit it and quit it. Also, yes, a little."

"Well, you can make assumptions, but how about you let me show you that that's not me."

I bit my bottom lip. "Sorry. I'm having a hard time believing that."

His grin was quick and showed off just how boyish he could look. "Well then, seeing is believing. Come on. I'm pretty sure you got up early to prep for this morning. And you look worried, so you're probably concerned about your former client. And if I know you, you started the background checks on your potential new clients already. And I can tell by the slight tremor in your hand you probably aimed for the liquid breakfast of just coffee and haven't eaten any solid food all day. Am I right?"

I shuffled my feet. "There's no need to see so clearly."

"Oh, I see you clearly, Sparrow Bridges. Now it's time for you to see me. Are you coming?" His grin was slow and sexy.

He stood and then reached out a hand for mine. I could've held back. Insisted on working. But instead, I placed my hand in his. It felt good. For the first time since I'd left the palace, I didn't feel quite so anxious. And I hated that feeling. I just wished I was able to settle my nerves on my own. But there was something oddly calming about Breck. I didn't have to be anything else other than who I was. And that made it easy. And the moment his much larger, warm hand clasped over mine, his features relaxed. His grin was easier, and then he leaned forward and kissed me on the forehead. "See, not so hard. Now come on, let's go eat."

I wasn't sure exactly what Breck meant when he said he was going to take me out to lunch. I expected some palatial scenario. On the beach, something fancy, flashy maybe.

The spot *was* on the water, but it was on the river, not the beach. And it was gorgeous, but there was nothing fancy about it. When he'd led me to the sleek black Maserati he drove, my mind had set all kinds of expectations that were nothing like the seafood joint we were at now. That was literally its name, The Seafood Joint. "I hope you like fish."

"This is great."

"It's my favorite. The chef's father is from Alden. His mother was from Ghana, so they do all kinds of delicious toppings and spicy things with their fish. It's delicious."

"Oh, wow. Okay. Not what I expected."

He laughed. "What, you thought I would glitz and glamor you?"

"Well, I'm not opposed to this, but I kind of did think that."

"Ah, to be underestimated."

I winced. "I'm sorry. That's not what I meant."

He shook his head. "No, it's not on you. That's on me. I have my own shit going on. But I know what people think. I'm a bit of a handful, a pain in the ass. Playboy, never serious, all that. It has been true in the past, but it's not necessarily true now."

I smiled at him. "Honestly, you're different than I thought you were."

"You know what? I'll take it. You ready to eat?"

"Tell me what's good."

Lunch was fun. My sinuses had cleared, and my nose had run from all the spices, but it was all delicious. After we finished eating, Breck led me hand-in-hand along the river on the promenade, pointing out land-marks as we walked. Then he asked, "So are we going to talk about this?"

I adjusted my sunglasses so he couldn't see my eyes. "Talk about what?"

"Wow, I thought I was cagey. This thing that's happening with us?"

Out of an abundance of caution and ingrained wari-ness, I furrowed my brow. "There is a thing?"

He chuckled. "Well, there is for me. And I thought there was for you. Maybe I was wrong?" He stopped walking and turned me to face him. "I know what I seem like. I also know you have good reason to question my judgment, my motives, what I want. But seeing you hurt the other day didn't sit well with me. And you are on my mind all the damn time. Constantly, actually. It's a little annoying because you distract me. I have goals and things I'm trying to do, and there you are. Because you'll smile or give me shit or say something really insightful, make me stop and think for a minute. And just so you know, with you, I'm not hit it and quit it."

"I thought we agreed you were going to stop saying that."

He flashed his grin. The one that made me melt on the inside even though I knew I should be shoring up the walls and defenses of my heart. "You agreed. I didn't. I kind of like it."

"Please don't."

"Hit it and quit it."

I rolled my eyes. "You're impossible."

"That's true. But I'm possible for you."

"Oh my God, the corny jokes."

"So, what do you say, Sparrow. Give a weary prince a chance?"

I shook my head slightly. "What am I going to do with you?"

"Well, we could start with kissing. But since we're in public, we'll want to keep anything more risqué to the car."

"You're not afraid of paparazzi?"

"Didn't you know they've been banned inside the city limits of Alden? You can take photos. You just can't actually get paid for them. Any photos found on the streets of Alden that are sold will immediately be removed."

"Wow."

"Yes, a little rule that helps us move around a bit easier."

"That explains why most people have left you alone today."

"None of our press will dare intrude unless it's a

sanctioned opportunity. Obviously, we can't stop the random lookie-loo, but at least they won't get paid by our papers for the images. Papers around the world I can't control. But the ones in Alden, yes."

"Wow."

"Don't think I haven't noticed you haven't given me an answer yet."

"Can I be honest?"

"Are you ever anything but?"

I had to grin at that. "No, never. I just... I'm worried. And I'm scared. And I want you so bad it hurts. And I know *I'm* going to get hurt."

"I promise not to hurt you. And I know that you have no reason to believe me. If there was something I could give you to show that I was serious, I would. But for now, maybe just have a little faith."

I searched his gaze. Bright blue eyes twinkling back intently on mine. "I want this."

"Then let's at least give it a shot."

"You sure you're not going to get bored?" I asked apprehensively.

"Is that what you think?"

"Well, I'm kind of straight and narrow. My biggest concern right now, you know, besides not getting killed, is doing a good job so I can impress my boss. He gave me a chance when no one else would. So I want to make sure that I make him proud."

He smiled. "And you will. I have full faith."

"How can you have that?"

"Because I know you. Even if you think I don't see, I do."

I cocked my head and gazed up at him. "You do, don't you?"

"I've seen the footage of your attack." He winced. "I still hate that I wasn't there, but I've seen it. I watched you fight for your life. And beyond being angry, of course, I was so incredibly awed by everything that you did. Everything you are. You are amazing to me."

"You know how to turn a girl's head, don't you? Using all those words. Make a girl feel sexy, why don't you?"

He winked. "That's the plan."

"You're sure?"

"If it helps, I'm terrified too. Because one of these days, I'm afraid I'm going to disappoint you."

"Then how about we don't hurt each other, and we don't disappoint each other. Will that work?"

He tugged me close and leaned down, his lips hovering just over mine. "I promise if you promise."

"I promise." And then his lips slid over mine, and my bones turned to jelly.

Chapter 13
SPARROW

The beginning of the end...

"I DON'T LIKE IT."

Breck shifted the hair off the nape of my neck and planted a lingering kiss along my skin, sending shivers down my back.

I was going over the schematics of our route one more time. Instead of waiting for Nix to come after me, I was going after him. It should be quick and surgical. Something about the plan and the timing seemed too easy. I'd gone over it so many times, but something in my gut just said this wasn't going to work.

Breck was doing his level best to distract me. "Oh, really? You sure about that? Because the past few days have shown that when I kiss your neck like that, you do, in fact, like it."

He nipped my skin then, and I shivered. "You know full well I like you kissing me. It's the plan. It's making me uncomfortable. I don't know... Something's off."

"I know something's off." I turned around slowly in his arms, and he leaned down to place a soft, lingering kiss on my lips. "Just let Wilder give you the men."

"Breck, we've been over this. He's given me two of his guys already. I think it's plenty. I'll be there. Niko too. We'll keep it tight. In and out, pick him up. Everything's going to be fine, I promise."

He ground his teeth and pushed to his full height, forcing me to crane my neck to stare up at him as I continued. "Don't be like this. You know I can do this."

The muscle in his jaw ticked. "Forgive me if I don't want the woman I—" He stopped abruptly.

I frowned. "The woman that you what?"

He cleared his throat. "You know that I don't do this, right?"

The pit in my stomach fell a few more feet. "Do what?"

He shook his head. "Do this. Relationships. Let myself get close to someone."

I sighed. "Is that what we're doing? Having a relationship?"

More ticking in the jaw, and this time he crossed his arms. I could physically see his shields going back up. Well, tough titties. I wasn't exactly here for the vulnerability and broken-heart shenanigans either. "Sparrow. We've been through this. That's what I'm trying to do here. Probably not well, and I warned you I wouldn't be great at this. But I am trying."

I forced my muscles to relax. He was trying. He was saying the right things and going through the right motions. They might not be perfect, but I had to accept them as they were. Because I wanted him. But shit, I was terrified. What if this *was* real? An actual real relationship. Could it even be that? Was either of us capable of *being* more, of giving *more*?

"I just... I'm worried about you. This doesn't feel good."

I pushed to my feet, but he didn't back away. The tight confines forced my breasts to push up against his chest. "It doesn't feel good for me either. You don't think I'm scared?"

His brow furrowed. "You don't look scared. You look *contained*. As per usual. And believe me, I have full faith in you. I believe that you can do anything. If you wanted to, you could move a mountain. And I would be right there supporting you. I just don't want you to break every bone in your body as you move that mountain." He was so warm, and he smelled so damn good. The scent of sandalwood wrapped around me, infusing my whole body with his scent, like he'd marked me. Like I would never be able to walk the earth again without smelling his scent lingering on my skin.

"You believe in me?"

His nod was firm. "Absolutely and unequivocally. I want you to be careful. And I know you hate it, and I'm not that guy, so I'm not going to tell you what to do, or go behind your back to my brother and force Wild to give you more men, or try and tell you how to do what I know you're good at. But, for the love of God, I can ask you to be careful. As someone I care about, which is, let me point out, a very limited list. Before you, that list was three. Now it's four. Four and a half if you count Kannon. The jury's still out on him."

My lips quirked up in a smile. "That's the thing, Breck. You pretend you don't care, but you do. You care about your people. I see it. You care about your employees. I've seen how you worry about the bottom line, what that means for them. You could easily sell your company for millions, but you don't because, in that scenario, only you make out like a bandit. Your employees would be left with barely anything. And that wouldn't sit right with you. I know you, Breck Waterford. I can see you."

He shifted on his feet, and his gaze slid away. "You know that makes me uncomfortable."

"Unfortunately, you see me too."

"Yes, I do. And I know better than to tell you what to do, but please for the love of Christ, get more men. *Take more men.*"

I knew what he was trying to say. I knew why he was trying to say it. I knew that he cared about me. I just also knew that this needed to be meticulous, with the precision of a surgeon's blade. If we went in with too many men, Truman Nix might get tipped off, and if he saw us coming, he might escape. Any manner of things could go wrong. And I couldn't have that.

"How about this. If I get that feeling, the weird anxiety I can't name, I promise I'll pull out. The guys and I *will pull out.* I will let you and Wild do what you want and put more security on me. I will call Kannon."

His brows popped. "What?"

I shrugged. "Yeah, yeah, I know. I swore I wouldn't call him. But if it comes to that, I will."

"You're sure?"

I knew what he wanted to hear, that I would absolutely call Kannon. And I planned to, unless I determined it was more dangerous for Kannon to be here. And by extension, more dangerous for London. But for now, I nodded. "Yes. So please, can I do my job?"

I could tell he was grinding his teeth, but he nodded. "I'm not sure I like this."

"You already said that."

"No. This whole compromise thing. I'm not used to it," he pouted.

I looped my arms around his neck, then pressed a kiss to his lips. "Well, the good news is, now that you've compromised, I will reward you."

He smiled. "Oh?" His hands slid around my waist and down to my ass. "How much time do we have left before you need to gear up?"

I laughed. "We don't have that much time."

He placed a finger on my lips. "Then shush. My turn. My turn involves lots of kissing. I mean, if you can be very quiet, my turn will also involve my cock inside of you. Ever had a quickie on your desk?"

I laughed. "No. And Niko's right outside. So are James and Adam, the guys Wilder sent over. I cannot shag you in my office."

His gaze grew dark then. "Yes, yes you can."

"I have to gear up. Strap on my weapons. I can't be all jellied out because you've sapped my energy."

"Yes, you can. Like I said, shush. I need to put my tongue and my fingers and my dick somewhere very, very fun. And you have to stay very, very quiet."

"Breck," I said in a warning, but he was already leaning down, his hands sliding up my back to the nape of my neck, angling me just how he wanted as his hands fisted in my hair.

"Like I said, be quiet now. If I only have five minutes, I need to work fast. And I don't normally do anything fast, so I'll need to concentrate and so will you. Now, sit on your desk and open your thighs."

Well, one thing I knew for certain; Breck was very, very talented with his hands and his mouth, and, well, his dick. And five minutes later, true to his word, he'd watched me gear up. And he'd relegated himself to being my guy in the van, which I knew had to be hard for him. I was grateful though. I tapped my ear as we drove up along the industrial road toward the warehouse and parked the van just at the ledge that let us approach the warehouse from the back. "Comm check."

Niko tapped his. "Roger."

James and Adam verified their comms were working as well. We were all geared in black, pistols in our holsters. I had an additional knife at my ankle. Niko had his long-range gun. James and Adam had that hard edge in their eyes, like military men well accustomed to walking headfirst into danger. And they were ready. Ready to walk by my side and possibly get shot in the process.

Stop it. That little voice inside my head still screamed that something wasn't right. I only had half my team, barely. Breck was good. He was very, very good, and I trusted Niko with my life. And if Wilder had provided me with men, I knew they would die to protect me. But it wasn't about that.

I just couldn't shake the feeling. The feeling that Breck was right. Still, though, I met each of my guys' gazes, brusque nods were exchanged, and then we all synchronized our watches. "Remember, in and out. Given the guard watch that they have, we know the exact timing of the shift change, so in and out. No elimination. Capture the target, bring him in. If something goes wrong and we have to engage, remember to injure, not kill."

Niko sighed. "Always with the no killing. You know it's more fun when you kill them, right?"

I sighed. "Niko."

He raised his hands. "Okay, okay. I hear you. But what if I shoot a guy in the balls? Does that count as killing?"

I sighed. "Seriously, Niko?"

He rolled his eyes. "All right, all right, fine. I'll go for the kneecaps."

The van door slid open. Niko hopped out. Next was James, and after him, Adam. When I went to launch myself out the open door, Breck dragged me back by the scruff of my neck and then leaned in close to my face, his lips an inch from mine. "I swear to God, if you die on me, I will be very, very pissed off."

I leaned in and gave him a quick brush of my lips. "I'm not going to die. Besides, you already gave me an excellent sendoff. Left me wanting more. So I'll be back for that at the very least."

"You'd better be."

With another quick kiss, I hopped out of the van, shutting the door quietly and then joining my team at the tree line.

With a series of hand gestures, I pointed Niko to his position and signaled the other two to follow me. We had cover from the trees to a certain point, and then we would be in the open for a hundred meters down the ravine.

But Niko was there and ready to provide all the cover we would need.

At the edge of the ravine, I looked down. Niko's voice was clear. "Ready, boss."

"All right, on my mark."

James and Adam were like silent sentries, saying nothing but moving as I moved. Like shadows that were permanently attached and not subject to the whims of the sun. We moved as a unit. At the very lip of the ravine, James went first, and I tumbled after him, sprinting as fast as I could move. Behind me, Adam's feet were the barest hint of a whisper. Silent. Deadly. I knew Niko had my back. I knew Breck was on overwatch. I was safe. I was protected.

So then why do you feel so goddamn uneasy?

We made it down the ravine. Ten meters, twenty meters, thirty meters, forty. At the last ten meters, a whisper of death skipped up my spine, and I tapped my comms unit. "Breck, anything?"

"No. All clear."

We sprinted behind one of the trucks parked at the edge of the property, and I panted, "Niko, you see anything?"

Niko's voice was low. "No. Nothing. Not even the guards. They're not due out for another minute, but I see no movement in the windows. Zero."

I cursed under my breath and then turned to the guys. Even though my senses screamed that I was walking into a trap, I had no choice. I had to keep moving. "Okay, let's roll."

We skirted around the trucks through the parking

lot until we were at the shadow of the building in a tight formation, weapons drawn, eyes on a swivel. I could practically feel Niko at our backs. I could feel Breck watching out for us. But still, something didn't feel right. Something didn't feel safe. Something still felt off and... *wrong.*

James set the charges for the back door, and we took cover, lining our bodies up behind the dumpster. With a silent *one, two, three* count, we blew the doors and then we breached. Smoke clouded our vision as we stepped in, weapons drawn, ready, adrenaline pumping and flowing through our veins, but we were met with no resistance. Not a single guard. Not a single bullet. The room felt empty, dank, dark. Adam had his hand on my shoulder, and James had a hand on his, and then we paused. Something sounded like a *tick, tick, tick.* Not like a watch timer, but like something rattling against something else.

And the next thing I heard was Breck's voice in the comms. "Shit. Abort. Abort. Sparrow, get out of there now. *Now.*"

I knew there was no way Breck was going to abort unless it was urgent. I didn't even think. I trusted him implicitly, at the very least with my life, if not with my heart. And we booked it out. We'd only made it as far as that first room, but I could feel it... death trying to climb up our spines. James was out first, then Adam. And then there was heat at my back, and I was going airborne as my teeth rattled and my back burned. We'd walked into an ambush. A trap. They'd known we were coming. Anticipated our every move. We'd been nothing but sitting ducks. And I'd almost gotten my team killed.

Chapter 14

BRECK

It wasn't supposed to be like this.

"PLEASE DON'T LOOK at me like that," Sparrow whispered, as I looked up at her, my heart racing.

"Like what?"

"Like I'm going to be blown up at any minute. I'm fine. I didn't get hurt too badly."

Not this time.

"I know you didn't..."

"And yet you're looking at me that way. Instead, you should be looking at me as if I was the one that sent you into that place. Oh, wait. That *was* me."

My heart clenched, and I let out a slow breath. I

kept seeing Sparrow on the floor, bloody, calling out for help. It wasn't her fault that her job put her in positions like this. But hell, I'd already lost my parents. Almost lost London. I didn't know what I'd do if I lost Sparrow too. "Sparrow."

"Don't, Breck. Not right now."

"Talk to me then."

"About what? What do you want, Breck?" She bit out the words then pressed her lips together, schooling her features.

"Sparrow."

"Do you really want to do this? Because I'm not sure I want to. What do you want to talk about? Maybe the fact that I almost got my team killed? How about that?" She was so calm as she spoke, but I knew she had to be hurting beneath the stoic exterior. I had to find a way in; I just wasn't sure she'd let me.

I moved forward so that I was in her space, and she raised her chin at me, glowering as I spoke. "Sparrow, it wasn't your fault."

"For somebody who is heir to the throne, you sure do not understand what it means to give orders. Because whatever order I give is what my men need to follow. Therefore, whatever happens afterward is on my shoulders. Maybe you don't understand," she said after a moment, narrowing her eyes at me. "Maybe it's only

Roman who understands. You don't get to give orders, do you?"

I ignored the barb because I knew she was hurting. And she was right. Roman did give orders. He did work with the council. I was just the spare. And yet, it didn't matter in that moment. The only thing that mattered was Sparrow, and maybe that should worry me, but it didn't.

"Sparrow, you don't have to blame yourself. You had intel, and it didn't pan out the way you needed it to, but everyone's fine. You're fine. I'm fine. We made it out."

She searched my face, her eyes wide. "Why are you acting as if you weren't part of this? As if I hadn't almost hurt you too?"

I met her gaze and slowly brushed my thumb along her lips. She smiled at me and then softened almost immediately, as if she couldn't figure out what she was supposed to be thinking. Good, because I didn't know what I was supposed to be thinking either.

"It's not your fault."

She shook her head. "That's the thing, Breck. It is. It was my decision, and I'm dealing with the consequences."

"But the consequences are only that we're still looking. Nix isn't going to be in hiding for much longer." I practically growled the words.

"And how is it you seem to know this?" she asked, clearly not believing me. Well, I didn't know if I believed myself either.

"Because I'm that good at my job. There's no way I'll let that man hide for long. He doesn't get to. Not after what he's done to you." I paused. "And everyone else."

"What am I supposed to do with you, Breck?" she asked, her breath soft against my lips.

Hell, I didn't know what to do, what to say. How could I be falling for her? I wasn't supposed to want this. I wasn't supposed to want *more.* I didn't get more.

But looking at her right then? At the way that her shoulders dropped ever so slightly, as if she could relax in front of me, undid me. How was I supposed to remain stoic against a woman who was so strong, so vibrant, and yet could peel away the facade of who she needed to be for others when she was in front of me?

I was falling for her strength, for the way that she saw me.

Because I wasn't just that playboy prince to her anymore, and I didn't know what to do with that.

"Why don't you let me take care of you for once?" I whispered.

"You always take care of me," she grumbled.

"Maybe I just need to not think for now, so let me take care of you."

"I think that can be arranged," I said, and then I lowered my lips to hers. Could I want more? No, I couldn't let myself think that. But maybe, *maybe* if I pretended just a little bit. After all, I was quite good at pretending. And I had to trust that she wouldn't leave or that I wouldn't watch her end up on the wrong side of a bullet or a bomb because of her job.

I wasn't sure how I was supposed to do that. She tugged on my belt loop, and I groaned into her, pushing away thoughts of what could happen and what could be. They weren't going to help anybody.

Instead, I kissed her again, tasting her, needing her more.

"I need you," she mumbled against my lips, and I was completely undone.

She didn't need anyone, a refrain she had said more than once. Yet here she was, needing me? How was that possible? How had this happened? But I couldn't focus on the whys, not when I needed to focus on the now.

So I kissed her harder, tugging on her hair slightly so I could move her head to the side. I latched my lips on her neck, and she groaned into me, her hands sliding down my back. She moaned again, and I moved my mouth up to bite her lip. She grinned, and I smiled back before taking her mouth again. In this, we were one, neither of us worrying about the past or future. Only worrying about what we had in each other's arms right then.

There was no duty or power or struggle. Just the two of us. And I had to remember that.

We were in my foyer, the one just for me and not other guests, the one right next to my bedroom. And I wasn't sure I could even wait long enough to get her to bed. Instead, I tugged at her shirt, and she smiled up at me before slowly raising her arms.

"Look at you, being all submissive," I said, winking.

She narrowed her eyes and nearly lowered her arms. But I gripped her wrists in a gentle hold so as not to hurt her and kept her arms above her head. I moved her back two steps, and her shoulders were pressed against the wall. She let out a sharp intake of breath, and I used the movement to capture her lips in another kiss.

"You are playing on dangerous ground," she muttered.

"Always," I said with a smile. And then I kissed her again.

Her breasts arched into me, and I moved back to gently cup one in my free hand. My other hand still bound her wrists, keeping her steady. She raised a brow at me, and I brushed my thumb along her nipple through her shirt and her bra.

"I can already feel how hard you are for me," I muttered.

"I thought that was my line," she said, pressing the softness of her belly to the ridge of my erection.

"Touché."

I kissed her again, and then I tugged her shirt out of her pants and slowly pulled it over her head. She kept her wrists above her head for me, and I kept that moment of trust between us, knowing if I screwed up here, she'd never forgive me. And I would never forgive myself.

"I want you," I muttered.

"Then you have me."

But could I have you forever?

I didn't ask that aloud. I didn't even let myself truly think it. Because I wasn't the prince of forever. I couldn't be. And yet, I wanted to be. For her. There was something wrong with me, but I didn't care, not right then. Instead, I kissed her again, and then lowered my lips down her neck, leaving gentle brushes and wisps of muttered words. She ground against me, and I moved to her other collarbone and then over her chest, in between her breasts. I undid the clasp that nestled between the gentle slopes of her breasts, and her bra fell away. I lowered my hand from her wrists, and let her arms fall softly, as I didn't want to hurt her. When she rotated her shoulders back and her bra fell to the ground behind her, I grinned at the movement, but my gaze was only for her breasts. Lush, tight brown nipples against honey-brown skin. She was gorgeous, and at least for now, she was all mine. I lowered my head and sucked one turgid nipple into my mouth. She gasped and slid her fingers into my hair. She tugged slightly, and I took that as an excuse to suck harder.

I twisted my lips and sucked so hard I knew she'd ache in the morning. But every time she moved, her nipples pressing against her bra, she would think of me. So I sucked again. And then I let go with a satisfying pop before moving to her other breast.

"It's too much, prince."

"Breck," I muttered against her soft skin. "My name is Breck."

I looked up at her then, and she met my gaze. "Breck. It's almost too much."

"Almost, but not enough," I whispered, and then I went back to kissing her sweet breasts.

I kept kissing down her skin as I lowered myself to my knees and licked and kissed my way along her stomach. She moaned and writhed in front of me, but I pressed her hips against the wall, careful of her injuries, her luscious ass giving her cushion.

"Breck, I'm already wet enough, and you haven't even taken my pants off."

"Really? Well, this is something I'm going to have to see." I undid the button of her pants as she toed off her shoes. And when I tugged her pants over her ass and down to her thighs, I looked at those lacy panties in front of me and inhaled.

"I smell you. All wet and hot. And just for me."

"You're on your knees in front of me, Breck, what else are you expecting?" she asked, her voice a throaty purr.

"I'm expecting you to scream," I said, and I lowered my face, stuck my nose in between her thighs, and inhaled again.

"Breck—" she said, shocked, and I chuckled roughly before pulling her panties to the side and licking her.

She clamped her thighs around my shoulders, and I grinned, before slowly tracing my finger along her wet lower lips.

"Well then, look at you, all wet and glistening."

"Jesus," she muttered.

"No, still just Breck," I said, and she tugged at my hair playfully. I lowered my head and sucked her clit into my mouth. She practically shot off the wall, and I used my free hand to keep her there before I sucked and licked and speared her with one finger.

"Look at you, all tight and ready for me. Am I going to stretch you, baby?"

"You know you will. Did you want me to say you have a big cock? Because I told you that before."

"A man always likes to hear compliments," I said, before I went back to licking between her legs. I licked, and I sucked, and then I spread her before me, pushing her panties to the side, as I looked at the feast in front of me.

"I can't wait to fuck you," I muttered.

"Then you should get to it," she purred in reply.

"I will, soon." And then I slowly worked my finger back, watching her face as her eyes widened.

"What do you think you're doing?" she muttered, but it didn't sound like a warning, almost like a need.

"Just teasing, testing," I whispered, and I slowly played with her, using her own juices to keep her wet and yielding.

She let out a soft gasp as I entered her with one finger, her gaze widening.

"Maybe later," I muttered before lowering my head, sucking on her clit, and using my thumb and finger to pleasure her both ways. She came with a scream, exactly what I wanted, my name and not prince on her lips.

When she finished bucking, I pulled away and lowered her on her stomach to the floor, placing her on the ultra-soft carpet so she wouldn't be hurt.

"My God," she moaned as I ripped her panties off, the lace tearing at the seams.

"I'll buy you new panties," I muttered, pulling my shirt over my head. I fumbled at my belt, and then my pants. The need was too great. I could barely breathe, barely think. She pressed into me, her ass sliding along my length, and I groaned.

Then I remembered a condom, and I cursed under my breath. I reached around to my pants pocket and pulled out the condom, and Sparrow took it from me as she rolled to a sitting position.

"My turn," she muttered, before rolling the condom down my length. She squeezed the base of my dick, cupping my balls, and I hovered over her, ready to come at one touch.

"Dear God, if you do that again, I'm going to die."

"Aw, don't do that, I just need you inside me."

"That I can do," I muttered. Then I positioned her on her hands and knees again softly on my carpeted floor, and lowered myself at her entrance.

"Inside me," she muttered. "Please."

"You never have to beg," I whispered. "Never. You tell me what you want, and I'm yours."

Her eyes widened as she looked over her shoulder. She gave me a strange look, and I knew I might've said too much, so instead of worrying about what she was going to say, I lowered my mouth, kissed her hard, and thrust into her balls deep in one solid movement. She pulled her mouth away, shouting in bliss, her fingernails digging into the carpet. But I didn't give either one of us time to think. Instead, I fucked her hard into the floor, pummeling into her as both of us shook with need. I was afraid I was going to hurt her, and that was one thing I promised I'd never do, so I pulled out of her. She gasped, and I rolled to my back before I tugged her over my waist.

"Fuck me, Sparrow. Show me exactly how you ride."

She pushed her hair back from her face, licked her lips, and rolled onto my dick. I gripped one hip, using my other hand to cup her breasts, playfully plucking at her nipples. She rode me with abandon, and both of us were breathing hard, each of us a sweaty mess as she lowered herself to me. I licked her nipple and then bit at her neck before I took her mouth. I pumped into her, as hard as I could, both of us leaving bruises, and when she shook, her pussy clamping my cock in a vice, I came right with her, not able to hold back anymore.

But thankfully, her mouth was on mine, and I couldn't say the words that had popped into my mind.

Because they would have been a mistake.

I couldn't love this woman. Not after such a short time.

But as she shook on top of me and pulled away, her eyes wide, glassy, and yet filled with something I couldn't read, I knew I was a lost cause.

I was falling for my protector, my Sparrow, and no matter what, I knew one of us was going to get hurt in the end.

And oddly enough, I didn't think it was going to be her.

Chapter 15
SPARROW

What happens when he's coming for you?

IT WAS A LONG, keening moan that woke me.

My name on Breck's lips. Like he was in agony. He twitched then his arm locked tight around my waist. I knew what he was dreaming of. The explosion. Me. The attack. The trap we'd walked into because I had been too eager. Too desperate to put this to bed. Too willing to walk in headfirst and prove to myself that I deserved to lead this team. Like a fool. I was lucky all I got was a slight concussion and some minor first-degree burns on my back. That explosion had been meant to kill me.

Luckily, Niko had been safe. And Breck. Fuck, what

if I had let him walk in with me like he'd wanted to? If I had taken his advice and gotten more men as he'd requested, how many would I have lost?

I shuddered, and Breck just held on tighter. His arm was like a vice, and then he murmured, "Sparrow."

It was only after he quieted that I eased out from under his hold. On the floor, I found the shirt he'd ripped open in his eagerness to get to me. His eagerness to touch me, make love to me, to forget that only a week ago he'd torn out of the van, giving no shits about his own safety. And he'd come running for me, putting himself out in the open.

Niko told me I had been out cold. I'd been less than thrilled that he'd endangered himself, of course, knowing full well that he wasn't supposed to be doing that. That wasn't our deal.

Now, he made love to me constantly. Like a man desperate to prove something, or a man who knew he was working on borrowed time.

You are *on borrowed time. It's not a good idea for you two to be together. You're too combustible.*

I was the careful, methodical one. He was pure impulse. But that day when he'd begged me to be careful, begged me to stay safe, to ask for more help, had I been the impulsive one?

After rolling up the sleeves and buttoning a couple

of the buttons of his shirt, despite my height, the shirttail still came down to my lower thighs, and I strolled out to the balcony overlooking Alden. The mountain view was spectacular down to the river, and the city lights twinkled. I loved this view. I loved Alden, and I was fighting to be able to stay in my new home. I hated bullies, and I refused to be chased from my home. But I worried how long this thing with Breck could last, especially if he was careless with his own life. *Because of me.*

Because of you.

With a glance back at the bed, I saw that he was still sleeping, so I went into the living room, grabbed my laptop, and took it back out to the balcony with me. I had missed something. At the very least, I'd missed Truman Nix being onto me. Because while I was watching him, he'd been watching me. So how long had he been in Alden? Had we seen him and his men only because he wanted us to? Had he been playing with us this whole time? Basically pulling an *Ocean's Twelve?* While we were busy chasing our tails trying to catch him, he'd been playing an entirely different game. One we didn't know the rules to.

Well, you'd better learn the rules... and fast.

We'd only been looking at immigration logs for a period of time in the last few months. But I went further back to a time where Kannon and London got married.

And then even still earlier when their love story went public. At that point in time, nothing had been decided. We hadn't known there'd be a Kannon Securities in Alden. Hell, Kannon and London hadn't even discussed where they'd live. But Kannon hadn't wanted her to leave her family, especially not with a baby on the way. Had Truman been watching us that long? Had he been planning since then? If so, he'd been directing this little circus freak show for months, not weeks.

Thanks to the software that Breck had lent me, I started scrolling through the passenger manifests, running the algorithm to root out all Aldean citizens. Residents. Those here on work visas. Anyone under the age of twenty to root out most of the students. Anyone with a student visa for longer than six months. Which still left a good deal of tourists. There was no point in trying to rule out the women, because even though it had been a man who attacked me in the parking lot that day, Truman could have anyone working for him. He was a misogynist, but there were plenty of female mercenaries who would do anything for money.

How the hell did I narrow this down?

"Why'd you leave bed?"

I whipped around with a startled shriek. "Jesus fucking Christ."

"I thought you were a security officer. Aren't you supposed to be stealthy and always aware?"

My breath was still tearing out of me in ragged pants, and I glowered at Breck. "You startled me. And those are ninjas. I'm not a ninja."

"Clearly. What are you doing? Why'd you leave bed?"

"I couldn't sleep."

Which was accurate. I wasn't going to add that he was having a fucking nightmare.

"If you couldn't sleep, I could help with that."

I gave him a soft smile. "I know, but you need rest too."

"What woke you? Tell me."

He bent down until his legs straddled the lounger I was on. "Nothing. I just couldn't sleep."

He sighed. "You know, for all your intelligence training and your extreme sassiness, you are a shit liar."

"It's nothing, Breck, really."

"When are you going to realize that I want to hear about it even if it is nothing?"

"You were having a nightmare," I said softly. I watched him warily as the realization dawned on just what he'd been dreaming about.

"Right. I was dreaming of the explosion."

"Once I was up, I was up."

"I'm sorry I woke you."

"It's not your fault. It's mine."

"What do you mean?"

"Well, if I'd listened, you wouldn't be having nightmares right now. I'd have Truman. Kannon and London would be able to come back."

"Is there room for another at this pity party, or is it just for you?"

"Go ahead, make jokes. But I'm being dead serious here. I could've gotten Wilder's men killed as well as Niko. They were just doing what their boss commanded them to do. You're a prince, and I could have gotten you killed too. So, what am I supposed to do with that? It's sitting heavy."

"And I'm telling you, they would have done it anyway. There's someone who is terrorizing you in that building."

"No, I don't think he was ever there. I think it was a trap from the jump."

"You and Niko have been on this all week. We followed the burner phones. There was a lot of activity coming from that building."

"Was it possible it was fake? Like for example if they anticipated Olly doing a search for that kind of activity?"

He frowned. "Not many people know how to do that."

"You know, I wouldn't have said Truman knew how to do it either," I shrugged, "but maybe he found out how. Maybe he's been planning this revenge for a long damn time. Because he's moves ahead of me in this game."

He sighed and then adjusted his position so that my feet fell into his lap. As he gently rubbed my arches, I moaned. "Oh God, that's not fair. I'm worried and tense. I think this state of mind helps my brain function."

"No it doesn't. Now, tell me what you were looking at."

I sighed and ran him through it. "What if he's been here for longer than we thought, or one of his men, or even a woman? It could be anyone. I'm trying to look farther into the past, exclude all residents, citizens, and students. Anyone who's been here longer than a year. But I'm..."

"So you're going back to the time when Kannon and London's relationship was made public? You think he's been here since then?"

"I don't know, but he's certainly been planning a lot longer than we thought."

"What are we going to do?"

"The only thing we can do; find a way to fight him.

We need to find out how long he's been here, who may have been watching us, to look and see if there's been any new staff hired at the palace. Staff meant for London. For the baby, maybe. Anyone who can get close enough to keep tabs on the family. I know you guys are generally pretty private, but your staff would know everything."

He rubbed his jaw. "If that's accurate, then Wild needs to be brought in on this."

"I'll call him in the morning. But right now, I need to figure out what the hell I'm going to do. I know I said I'd call Kannon back, but if Nix is this in tune with us, knows exactly where we've been and what we've been planning, then Kannon, and most certainly London, are in trouble if we bring them back home too soon. And right now, no one, I mean no one, knows where they've gone."

Breck frowned. "Well, Roman does, but Wild and I don't."

"That's the point. Even I don't know where they are specifically. The security protocol officers don't know, so right now they're safe. I worry that we have a breach, that someone is listening who shouldn't be, because no one should have known we were there."

"Even better, no one should have been able to predict your movements. I think he's been watching."

"I have an idea. But I don't think it's one you're going to like."

He put down one foot and picked up the other one, massaging the tension in the arch. Then he lifted my foot and leaned down to kiss one of my toes. "Sparrow. Let's just be clear. I can see the wheels turning in your brain right now. And that's a beautiful thing. But after the last time, your plan had better not involve using you as bait."

I bit my bottom lip. "Well, does it count if I don't tell you that it involves using myself as bait?"

"Absolutely not."

"Look, he wants me. He wants revenge. What if I give him me as a trade? You and Wild can arm me with all the latest tech and toys and support team as you can. But what if instead we just hand me over?"

He leveled a stare at me and looked furious. "Like I said, over my dead body is that ever going to happen."

And I knew in that moment that he would not let me go voluntarily. Which was why I was going to have to break his heart and go on my own.

Chapter 16
BRECK

The middle of the end doesn't have to be the end.

"LIKE I SAID, over my dead body is that ever going to happen."

As soon as I said the words, I knew they were a mistake. Those were exactly the wrong words to say to someone like Sparrow. She wasn't the person who would stand back and let someone else do what she thought was her duty. If somebody needed help, she would be right there. She would sacrifice herself, body and soul, to keep others alive, to keep them safe.

Her own safety be damned.

And it was one reason I loved her. It had taken me

too long to realize it. I had thought that our fighting with each other for so long was because of hatred, not a connection I had refused to see.

But I could not let her get hurt. And yet I didn't have any right to tell her how to do her job.

I couldn't.

And I couldn't watch her die.

But I had a feeling, no matter what I did, no matter what case came up, I would have to. Because she would die to protect those under her care, and I couldn't fault her for that, but I was sure I couldn't watch it happen.

"I'm going to pretend you didn't just say that," Sparrow said, her voice icy.

"Maybe I shouldn't have said it," I said softly.

"There's no maybe about it. You don't get to tell me how I live my life or how I do my job. I'm not like the little royal bunnies, or whatever the hell they're called. I have a job to do, and you're not going to hold me back."

"I didn't give a fuck about any of those 'royal bunnies' as you put it. *You* I care about."

"That's not even the point, and I shouldn't have brought it up since that's your past, not mine. The point is, you don't get to control me. You don't get to stand in the middle of my job and purpose and tell me what to do."

I bit my tongue before I said something I knew I'd

regret and took a deep breath. "I'm not trying to tell you what to do; I'm trying to tell you what *not* to do."

Sparrow just blinked at me. "That's a silly line from a movie that never made sense to begin with. This is my *job*, Breck. This is what I'm good at, what I'm trained for. Just because we've slept together doesn't give you the right to dictate what I do."

"You're going to get yourself killed, Sparrow! I can't watch you do that." My heart raced out of my chest, and Sparrow just stared at me.

"I know what I'm doing, Breck. You're not going to watch me die. I might get hurt. That comes with the job, but my death is not inevitable."

My hands shook and I let out a breath. "I can't watch you do this."

She studied my face again, her expression so shuttered I couldn't read her emotions. I hated when she did that. She was so good at protecting others that she pushed people away to make it happen. "What are you saying?"

"I'm saying that it's fucking hard to be in a relationship with you!"

She blinked, her mouth parting. "Fine. You don't have to be. There's no relationship. I get it. We'll fuck when we're in the mood. As long as you don't get to think you can tell me what my job is. I guess that means

I get to go out, hunt down the bad guys, and then come back and fuck you whenever I feel like it."

I growled, *literally growled.* "That is not what the hell I'm telling you."

"Then why don't you just spell it out for me."

"I don't know how to put it into words."

"You sure are good with your words when you're trying to get me into bed."

"Am I? Or are we just excellent at hiding from the situation. How about the fact that most of the time when we're together, it's *after* you almost get blown up, stabbed, or beat to within an inch of your life?"

She shrugged. "It's part of the job. And I'm damn good at it."

"You are. And that means every time I'm with you, I have to count the bruises, the cuts. And wonder if one day you're not going to come home."

"That's the job, Breck. Your job comes with paparazzi and people wanting to know every little thing about you. Your job comes with the secrets that you have. The fact that nobody seems to know that you're a brilliant person with so many patents it's insane. But nobody knows that because you hide it. That's your job. You let everybody see your public persona, and then you hide the rest. And I understand it. That you need to keep that part of you to yourself. I don't get why your family doesn't know, but maybe that's not my place. After all, we're not in a relationship."

"That's not what I'm saying, damn it. We *are* in a relationship."

"You could have fooled me, not according to what you're saying."

"Then just shut up and let me speak."

She raised a single brow. "You don't get to tell me to shut up. That's not what we do here."

I raised my hands. "You're right. I'm sorry."

"Breck, I don't understand you."

"I don't understand me either. But I refuse to wonder what's going to happen when one day you don't come back."

A single tear fell down her face, but she wiped it away quickly. That was my Sparrow. She didn't cry, really, didn't show her emotions. She only did sometimes for me, and usually, I figured it was an accident, as if she wasn't even sure she had bared any part of herself.

"I don't have a choice, Breck. This is my job. Sometimes I'm going to have to leave to take care of people, and you're going to have to let me."

"Sparrow," I whispered, not knowing where to begin.

"I can see it in your eyes that you don't want to let me go, but you're going to have to. I'm going to get hurt sometimes. It's my job to protect others, which means I get to stand in front of someone else's bullet. But if I do my job well enough, that bullet will never come. But I need to keep my mind in the game. I need to focus, and while I know that what we have could be good, I can't let it keep distracting me. So, it doesn't matter that I've fallen in love with you. I need to focus on Nix and exactly how I can protect my team."

I nearly staggered back at her words, and her eyes widened as if she hadn't even realized she had said them.

"Breck," she said, and I cut her off.

"You love me," I muttered.

"You're right. I do. I'm not going to lie to you. I never have. But I have a job to do, and you need to let me do it."

I looked at her then, and I knew I would never be able to hold her back. No amount of words or actions would do it. And the thing was, I didn't want to. Doing that would change who she was and hurt her irrevocably.

And I couldn't be the person who did that to her.

But I also didn't know who else I could be.

And so I moved forward, watched her as she watched me, and I lowered my mouth to hers. I brushed my lips along hers, the chasm in my heart deepening with each caress.

"I love you," I whispered.

Her eyes softened, and then I took a step back.

"I love you," I repeated. "But I can't watch you kill yourself."

And then I turned on my heel and walked away from the love of my life.

I had watched others die before, had nearly lost my sister and so many others.

And I couldn't lose her that way.

Even if I knew I was destined to be shattered in the end.

Chapter 17

BRECK

Parting is anything but sweet sorrow.

I'D CLOSED my door when I'd come into work. The act of doing so had sent pitying looks throughout my team. I only closed my door for important meetings or when my brother stopped by and acted the king he was.

Doing so today meant I didn't want to talk to anyone, but they already knew. My team had seen the pain and anger etched on my face even if I hadn't let anyone in on the secret. How were they supposed to know that I'd told the first and only woman I'd ever loved that I was so in love with her I couldn't be with her? They only saw parts of me, just like my family saw different parts, and the rest of the world and the women I'd fucked in my past saw the other slices of myself that I'd hidden away.

I'd let myself feel. I'd let myself open up to someone else, and look what it got me. Nothing but the shattered remains of my dignity and a cold slap in the face.

I might be the idiot for walking away or letting anything happen in the first place, but now I couldn't change my decisions. And I wasn't sure if I wanted to.

There was a soft tap on the door, and I looked up to see Jaye rocking from foot to foot. I did my best to school my features and not act like the ass I knew I was. I was their boss, their team leader. They didn't need to see me break down or scream and shout at the injustices of the world. They already knew them in their own ways.

"I'm sorry to bother you, but there are a few documents you need to sign before the weekend." She walked into my office carefully, as if I were a bomb about to explode, and I held back a sigh. She'd had that pitying glance for me when I'd first walked into the office, and I hadn't missed it. She'd hidden it quickly enough, but I knew she felt sorry for me—even if she didn't know all of the details behind it. No one did. Hell, I wasn't sure even if I did.

"You're not my admin, Jaye. Why are you dealing with paperwork? Where's Jason?"

Jaye sighed. "He went home with a toothache. He's now in the middle of a root canal with Alden's finest dentist."

I cringed. "Ouch. You all should have told me."

She gave me a look, and I sighed. "Just sign these. They are the preliminaries for the discussion if we're selling the new slice of the business or not."

I frowned as I looked over them. "I read these yesterday. Did I not sign them?" I looked up at her sigh. "I guess not. I seem to be dropping the ball all over the place. Okay, I'll look through these again and get them sent out. And I'll forward Jason's desk to mine and deal with the admin. You've all been working too hard to start taking more of his job on top of it."

Jaye shook her head, her dark hair falling over her face. "You work longer hours than any of us, plus you have your royal duties. We can all share the burden."

"Just send it over," I gritted out, then forced myself to calm down. "I have more time these days and don't mind the work. I'll get it done so Jason can rest." She met my gaze and I wanted to curse myself for adding that part.

Hell.

"Whatever you say, boss. Just... Just let me know if there's anything I can do." She paused and I looked up at her. "Olly and I have another meeting later, too. For the *thing*. If you want to know."

I set my jaw. "Thanks, Jaye. You and Olly do good work." At my tone she gave me another of those pitying looks, then slowly left my office, closing the door behind her.

I had work to do, code to write, and empires to sell. I didn't have time to wallow in my own demise. I'd been the one to put myself in this situation, and now I needed to deal with the consequences.

Even if every time I closed my eyes, I saw Sparrow's face.

And every time I took that next breath, I remembered almost losing her.

And then...I remembered that I'd walked away, losing her in the end anyway.

Sparrow

MY HEART THUMPING, I ran through the palace grounds. Hell, I barely let my car slide into park before

I'd thrown the door open, bolting my way to Wilder's office.

I ran through the main courtyard and skidded, almost missing my exit point.

In thirty seconds, I was at his door, banging wildly.

The low baritone sounded annoyed as he called out, "Open."

Breathless and panting, I shoved the door open and his brows immediately drew down. "Sparrow? What's wrong?"

"I'm sorry. I'm so sorry. I couldn't just call you. I had to show you."

I handed him over my phone. The text from the unknown number.

He frowned down at it. "What?"

I took my phone back and then scrolled to the right messages.

"That. 'If you won't do as I say, your new beloved home is going to get a facelift.'"

Wild cocked his head. "Who's this from?"

"I think it's from Nix. He's the one who sent men after me. He's the one."

"Okay, Nix. You and Kannon helped his wife, right?"

I nodded. "Yeah."

"Breck told me about it. Okay, so what does he mean by a facelift?"

"Keep reading," I panted.

His eyes scanned the myriad of texts. The demands, what was at stake if we didn't comply.

He rubbed at his chin. "He wants Kannon?"

I nodded. "Yes. And he blames Kannon for his wife leaving."

"Okay. These kind of people are never rational, but what does he think Kannon's going to fix?"

"Oh, Kannon's not going to fix anything. Scroll down."

Breck started scrolling and speed reading, and then his eyes went wide. And wider. And then I watched as he paled. "He set bombs around Alden?"

"Yes. He says he's got explosive devices laid out all around the city. He says if he catches wind of my team or anyone from palace security looking, he's going to detonate. If we do anything other than bring Kannon to him, he's going to detonate the bombs. I don't think he knows Kannon isn't in the country."

The litany of curses that tripped off of his tongue included ones I'd never even heard. "Sparrow, you can't give in to this."

"You think I don't know that? I need help. Otherwise this city, *this country*, is in grave danger. He's going to do something unforgivable, and I need to stop it."

Wilder furrowed his brow. "Okay, relax. I'm going to call Roman. We'll figure this out."

"You're not listening. If he catches wind of palace security knowing about this threat, he's going to detonate. I don't know where they are located, and I can't even have Olly hack their location, because he's not here."

His brow creased with worry. "Okay, just breathe."

Why was he so levelheaded? Didn't he understand what was going to happen? And that I felt at fault? "You are exceptionally calm."

"I'm intelligence. Do you know how many threats I see on a daily basis? The only way you think through something rationally is by remaining calm."

He was right. I need to relax, at least to take a deep breath. I couldn't think under stress.

"Okay, we'll get Ronan on the line. We need plainclothes elite officers to begin the searches. We can get the dogs going. There's a lot we can do to at least start combing the city. Systematically. We can do some aerial sweeps, get some drones. And it'll look like business as usual."

"I know you're trying to help, Wilder, and I appreciate it. I didn't know what else to do. This is the first time I've dealt with a threat of this magnitude, and I don't have any answers."

"You don't have to have the answers. You have a team, remember? Hopefully I'm on that team."

I sigh. "I'm just used to doing so much myself."

"Well, you don't have to anymore. You have backup. Look, I'll get my brothers, and we'll start figuring this out."

"We can't just give him Kannon."

"I know. First, I like the guy. Second, that would break London's heart. And finally, we don't trade lives, so that's not a thing we're going to do."

I chewed my bottom lip. "Unless."

He frowned. "There's no unless. There's no way we're doing that. We'll stop this from happening."

"What if there was a way to stop this from happening and let him *think* he was getting Kannon?"

He lifted a brow. "Talk fast, Sparrow. Something tells me we don't have any time to waste."

Chapter 18
SPARROW

They call it ice for a reason.

IT HURT. Having Breck walk away from me hurt like something with talons had burrowed into my chest, twirled around, then tried to claw its way back out again.

My brain tried to work out where everything had gone wrong.

You went wrong by falling for him. By losing focus.

Everything had seemed fine until the warehouse explosion. He'd been so supportive. I'd never in my life had someone back me up like he had over the last couple of weeks. But I couldn't do what he was asking. I couldn't walk away from this. Truman Nix was coming after my family and everything that was important to me. How could I just sit back and let other people die for me while I did nothing?

I knew he was worried, but I'd expected that he would understand why I had to be the one to solve this problem. But instead of understanding, instead of listening to me explain, he'd just walked away. So now I was alone... again.

"You got your head in the game?"

I glanced up at Niko. He was armed to the teeth with a long gun over his shoulder. We were situated in a van in the woods, half a kilometer out from the old Alden warehouse where we were meeting. During the week, it was still used as an old truck depot and offices for those in the warehouse district. It was deserted on the weekend though. Thank God for small favors.

Wilder had worked to sneak weapons packs around the building, each with a tiny GPS transmitter. We had matching receivers in our boots. Once we were close to one of the transmitters, our boots would flash rapidly.

"I'm fine."

The muscle in his jaw ticked. I'd never really considered Niko dangerous before, but I supposed that was because he was always on my side. "You are not fine. Stop that nonsense. Maybe now isn't the best time to be running headfirst into danger?"

Maybe he had a point. "What else am I supposed to do?"

"I don't know. Maybe saying 'don't run headfirst into danger' seems weird coming from me, of all people, I know. But I'm worried about you."

"I'm fine. You should know better, honestly."

His gaze narrowed. "Is that what you really think, or what you need to tell yourself so that you can function and do what we need to do today?"

"You don't need to head shrink me. I'm good."

Niko sighed and checked his weapons. "Look, you're tight. You're always tight. After all, you're Sparrow. You're the one who keeps us in line and makes sure that we have everything we need. You are always in control, which makes you a great operator. I trust you with my life. Hell, Olly can't even function without you. How he's managing back home now is beyond me. And I don't mean just as an operator, but as a friend too. But when it comes to relationships, it's not about being in total control."

"Is this really the time for this talk?" I frowned at him. "We have an asshole to catch."

He nodded slowly. "We certainly do. One who seems hellbent on killing you in particular. And the sad eyes you're giving me are throwing me off here. I think your head's not in the game today."

He had a point, but I wasn't telling him that. "I'm super tight. I'm the bait. Well, Kannon and I both are. And thanks to Wilder, I have a great Kannon decoy in place, so we're going to walk into that building and hand ourselves over. You and the rest of the team are going to neutralize the target and get any other innocents out of there as safely that you can."

"You know this is a dumb plan, right?"

I frowned at him. "Then why are you here?"

He chuckled at that. "Because we're a team. And you wouldn't be doing this stupid thing unless you thought it was really going to work. So of course I'm here. But your head's not in this. You went and caught a case of lovesickness. Which is cool. But if you can't even admit to yourself how you feel, you're going to stay distracted."

I sighed. "Jesus Christ, Niko. Fine, I fell in love or whatever. But he walked out on me, so it is what it is."

"Look, just try to put your emotions aside and focus on the plan. You get close enough to Nix and stab the fucker in the leg with the tranq dart. He goes down and you and the Kannon stand-in walk out safely. That's it. Easy peasy."

Why doesn't it feel easy? Everything had to go

perfectly. Wilder's Kannon impersonator was tall enough, and he was built like Kannon. Maybe a little leaner, but he'd do. He had the same dark hair, and we'd cut it in roughly the same style, although he'd be wearing a hood so he wouldn't be noticed right away. And maybe we'd get lucky and Truman Nix wouldn't remember the details of Kannon's face after two years. Either way, I'd work with what I had.

You have everything except Breck.

I still couldn't believe he'd walked away from me when talking me out of this didn't work. As if I had any other choice. I refused to let Kannon and London come back just to walk him straight into danger when I could stop it, when I could *do* something. And for all Breck's talk about how he believed in me and my ability, how could he not understand that I needed to do this?

Shake it off, focus. I inhaled sharply and leveled my gaze on Niko. "I'm good. I will fix my messed-up love life later."

If there *was* any way of fixing it. Because how could I be with someone who wanted me to be a different version of myself? I'd known we were different, and still, I'd let myself fall for him. I'd let myself dream about the possibilities. I had let myself *believe*. That's why it had hurt so much when he walked away. That's why I felt like I was being stabbed repeatedly between my ribs.

But Niko was right. I had to walk in there and follow the plan. Distraction would only get people killed.

We were half a kilometer from the meet point, where I and this poor guy—what was his name, Brighton? We were going to walk into a building knowing full well that the people inside it wanted to kill us. Inside, we would have no support. It would be the two of us, a tranq dart, a hope, and a prayer.

We wore normal clothes over our specially designed squirrel suits in case of emergency. In the platform lift of my boots were a tiny penlight, lock pick tools, and the syringe. Same for Brighton.

Niko started climbing out of the van. "All right, I'm going to head out and take position in the building across the way. If anything gets messy, head toward the south-facing side of the building with all the windows. Give me the signal, and I'll start shooting things that aren't you."

"I hear you."

That was Niko's job. Eyes in the sky. We'd let it play out as long as we could, because the target was Truman. And so far, he'd only sent his henchmen. If something went wrong and we needed a rescue, we'd go to the windows, and he would start shooting. We were going to be on the fifteenth floor, just barely high enough for the damn squirrel suits to work properly if we had to bail out one of the windows. The only disadvantage was that Brighton's hands would be cuffed. So if he got tossed out of the building, that was going to be a problem.

One step at a time.

An SUV arrived, and out climbed Wilder. I couldn't help it; my heart squeezed when I searched for Breck and didn't see him, but I focused on Wilder. "Your Highness."

He lifted a brow. "Oh, really. You're about to do something crazy, and now you're going formal with me?"

I shrugged. "If not now, then when?"

"Good point." His gaze searched mine. "Are you sure about this?"

"Like Niko, you worry too much. I'm coming back."

"Seriously. You've got that beacon in the sole of your shoe. You hit it if you get in trouble, and the cavalry comes running."

"You know you can't do that. He says he has bombs rigged. He'll level that building and three others in Alden, and we don't know which buildings."

"Listen, Breck's on it, okay? We'll figure out where the other bombs are located."

I was just going to ignore that twinge of my heart. "If you say so."

He placed a hand on my shoulder. It felt big and heavy. Similar to another hand, except this one was meant to reassure me. "Look, I don't know what happened. But he was a wreck the other night."

I shrugged. "None of it matters now. We have a job to do. Please tell me your team's good enough to find those other bombs, because I can't let him kill your man."

"That's not going to happen. Breck and his team are already searching."

"Are you sure about that?"

"I'm sure. In the meantime, we evacuated the buildings in Oldtown that are near the palace. You just have to walk in there and stall for time. Let him make some big villain speech."

I wrinkled my nose. "No one ever does that."

He laughed. "You'd be surprised."

How was it Wilder could be here and Breck couldn't be? "Okay. I guess this is it."

I started to march toward the SUV, and he stopped me. "Hey, Sparrow?"

"Yeah, Wild?"

"You'll be okay."

"Right. Of course I will." I really wanted to believe that.

He cleared his throat. "And just so you know, my brother loves you."

I squared my shoulders and jutted out my chin. "Well, he's got a funny way of showing it."

Wilder winced. "I don't think he can stand to see you walk headfirst into danger. Even if he knows you're right, that this is your job and it's what you're supposed to do. He loves you, so of course, he doesn't want this for you."

"Then we are at an impasse. Because this *is* my job, and I'm not changing. I'm not walking away. This is part of who I am."

"And I think he knows that. He just wants to be considered in your decision making."

I shook my head. "No. He wants me to only consider *his* decisions. And I can't do that."

Wilder sighed, but then he nodded. "Good luck, Sparrow."

"Thanks."

I climbed in the driver's seat of the SUV where Brighton was waiting in the back. My voice was low when I asked him, "Are you sure about this? You don't have to do this."

From the back seat, all I got was a *mm-hmm*.

I sighed. What did I expect him to say? I was quite possibly sending him to his death. At the very least, I was sending him into a hostage situation with nothing more than a tranq dart and his hand-to-hand combat skills. Oh, and Wilder had cuffed his hands behind his back and blindfolded him to make it look like I was delivering him to Nix against his will. Of course, he wasn't feeling particularly loquacious.

When we arrived, I parked the car in the designated spot I'd been told to use and then eased out before helping Brighton out of the back. We took the rear entrance that led to a basement and walked down a long hallway. Brighton's moves were quick and sure. As if he'd walked this very hallway more than once.

"Uh, Brighton. I don't know you well. And I know this sucks being blindfolded and led by someone you don't know or trust. But I appreciate it."

He shrugged.

"Right, not chatty, got it. But thank you anyway."

Another shrug, but this one felt more like acquiescence.

At a set of double doors at the end of the hall, we were met by two armed gunmen. A nice show of force. One of them said, "Stay right there."

I released Brighton and put both hands up. "See, we did exactly as we were told. Give us the locations of the bombs."

There was a low chuckle, and then I was shoved forward. Someone dragged Brighton behind me. *Fuck.*

The two of us were then shoved into the elevator. Brighton was shoved in so hard that he almost slammed into the far wall of the lift, and I said, "Hey, take it easy."

The guard didn't give a fuck. He just laughed.

I rubbed my hand over Brighton's back, and he tensed. I tensed too. "Are you okay?"

His nod was slow. "We'll get out of this."

The taller of the guards said, "Not likely."

The elevator dinged, and we were led out onto a mostly empty floor. It looked like maybe a company had occupied it recently, but it was now empty except for a few random desks and office chairs. There were two chairs in the middle of the room, and we were shoved toward them. I was slammed down hard, my butt nearly bouncing off of it. Same for Brighton.

The shorter of the guards said, "Oh, Mr. Nix has been looking forward to this. But first, I think he might have a few harsh words to say to you, Miss Bridges."

I flinched. The last thing I wanted Truman Nix to do was to view me as a woman in any way. That did not to bode well. "We're here. We held up our end of the bargain. If you don't hold up yours, the king and princes will come at you with everything they have. You'd best remember that."

A door at the far end of the room opened, and in walked Nix. "Well, well, well. Miss Bridges. Long time no see."

Jesus Christ, it was Truman. He walked close to me, but not close enough.

I could feel Brighton being tied to the chair behind me and struggling against his restraints. "Easy does it, Truman. You gave us your word. Keep it, or you're not making it out of Alden alive."

"Now, now, there's no need to threaten. I'll keep my word. Eventually."

I glowered up at him. "Now. You will keep your word now."

He pulled out his phone and made a call, giving two addresses. Then he ended the call.

I scowled at him. "Those are not the correct addresses."

"I have no intention of double-crossing you, Miss Bridges. Besides, I got what I wanted out of this deal— you and Mr. Adams here. I must say, it was very, very brave of you to offer yourself up as a sacrifice."

Behind me, someone tied my wrists to Brighton's. But then he worked his hand around and squeezed mine. Twice. That wasn't the signal. What was he doing?

And why did his hand feel so familiar? A shock of electricity zinged up my arm.

No!

That wasn't—I'd seen Brighton. They'd put a jacket and hood on him.

My brain wasn't processing right. It kept telling me that the man behind me wasn't Brighton at all, but the man I loved.

My senses told me that it was Breck behind me. And I didn't want to believe it.

Truman Nix came closer. So close that I could smell his too sweet breath. "God, I must say, Sparrow Bridges, you have proved most difficult to bring in. You've taken out several of my men. If it was possible that I could be impressed with a woman, I would be impressed with you."

I stared up at him. "Are you done being an asshole?" I knew I needed to buy time to give Wilder and his men the opportunity to verify the information they'd been given. In the comm device in my ear, Niko's voice was low but clear. "Eclipse. Eclipse. Eclipse. Decoys. All we found were decoys."

Behind me, whoever it was tensed because we'd been led astray. Led to believe that there were explosives in the city, and they were decoys. That meant we'd been had, and we were going to have to fight our way out of this.

Truman leaned in closer, too close. "You see, Miss Bridges, I'm starting to think that maybe we are exactly where we're supposed to be. You and me. My wife was weak, but you have proved a more than worthy adversary. A fight with you would be like fighting a goddamn Amazon. And God, I've got to tell you it makes my dick wet."

I flinched. "Where are the explosives? Are you sure you told us exactly where they all are?"

His smile was evil, all teeth, and it went perfectly with his rat-like eyes. "Now, did I say there were explosives, plural? Maybe there's just one. Now, your man Kannon here, he's going to die quickly, easily. But you, I think I'm going to keep you." He signaled to his men, and I knew that was our chance, our one and only shot.

"You're never going to make it out of here alive, Nix, and you certainly aren't going to have me. Thanks to your sex tape from a few years ago, I've seen the size of your equipment. I would rather die here than deal with a little dick. It's just not something I see in my future."

Fury flashed in his eyes, and he lunged at me. "What the hell did you say?"

With a flick of the wrist, the bonds broke on one of the

zip ties holding me, and I lunged for Truman. He clamored backward, tripping over his own feet. The problem was I'd lost the momentum. Behind me, Brighton, because I *had* to think of him as Brighton, was already working on his other zip ties. And then he yanked off his hood.

I should have felt shock. I should have felt surprise. I should have felt anything other than abject terror. "Jesus Christ, Breck, what are you doing?"

"Well, you weren't going to stop, so I had to come with you."

"You're an idiot."

"Possibly. But here we are."

To my left, I saw Truman pulling himself up. Reaching for a gun. Finally, I snapped the other zip tie from the chair. Then I was on my feet and launching myself at him while Breck had his hands full with the guards.

Truman shoved a foot out, kicking me hard in the sternum, and I fell backward.

And then he was on me. Fuck, he was heavy. It felt like he'd concentrated all of his body weight so that it centered on my lungs. When he wrapped his hand around my neck, I coughed as he said, "You stupid cow. I had plans for you. Great plans. But no, no. You had to fucking ruin everything."

Through clenched teeth, I bit out, "Fuck you."

"I know you'd like to, sweetheart. But, instead, you're going to die here."

I screamed and clawed at his hand.

Over to the side, I watched in horror as Breck fought off the two guards. In the flurry of fists and knees and elbows, his face was set in a grim line, ready and willing to do whatever it took.

I didn't have time to worry about him.

I had to deal with Truman first and get his damn phone so I could find out where the real explosive device was.

I raised my arm up over my head and then brought it down across his elbows, breaking the grip on my neck. The release was quick and sudden, and the rush of air made me gasp. "Jesus."

I didn't have time to rest, though, or time to breathe. I had to keep fighting. As he grasped for my hips to pull me down, I tightened my abs as if I was trying to sit up, and I wiggled back and forth out of his grasp. Once my legs were free, I kicked him in the face with all the force I could muster.

I shot to my feet and jumped on him, giving him no time to recover. With determination and rage I rarely ever let myself feel, I rained fists down on him, blow after blow. And when I knew those wouldn't be strong enough, I used my elbows.

I had to avoid his grip.

He was reaching for my neck again, and I knew I wasn't going to win this on pure strength. So I grasped his ears, picked up his head, and bashed it down into the floor. Once, twice. And then I pushed to my feet, aiming my knee at his chest. I let all my weight fall forward onto his chest and heard the satisfying crack of a rib.

Nix's eyes popped open as he wheezed, "Fuck you."

When he didn't pass out, I did it again. And finally, he groaned and stopped fighting.

Quickly, I checked for a pulse. He was still breathing. I pulled his phone out, grabbed for his hand, and used his thumb to unlock it then tapped my comms. "Eclipse. Eclipse. One active device here in the building. I need to go disarm it. Truman is down, incapacitated. Don't send anyone in. I'm sending Breck back out."

There was a crackle on the line, and then Wilder's voice rang in my ear. "Roger. We hear you loud and clear."

He'd known. He'd known Breck had come with me.

Damn it. I didn't have time to think about that.

I glanced up at Breck. And while he had two trained guards fighting him, he looked perfectly at ease. As if he did this kind of hand-to-hand combat all day, every day.

He delivered a roundhouse kick to the shoulder of one of the guards. His head snapped to the side, and he fell.

Breck swiped at the blood on his nose and then sent me a feral smile. "Go. Get to the bomb. I'll deal with this."

"You have to get out of the building."

"You worry about the fucking bomb. I have this. You do what you need to do."

I wanted to wait. I wanted to go to him and say the things that I couldn't say before. *I love you. I'm sorry. Thank you.* But there wasn't time for that.

Instead, I had to run. Because there were people counting on me to get this right.

I sprinted out the far door then swung to the right, following the locator on Nix's phone toward the stairs, climbing two at a time. I made it up another four flights, to the level just below the roof. Another left brought me to the room where the bomb should be located. I tried the handle, but it was locked. *Fuck, fuck, fuck, fuck.*

I pulled out my lock pick set, knelt down, and tried to stay calm. In my ear, Niko's voice was low. "Talk to me Sparrow."

"Oh, you know, just got to pick a lock."

He chuckled low. "You can do that in your sleep. Want me to time you? You'll go faster that way."

"Shut up, Niko."

But just hearing his voice and knowing he was okay and watching my back helped to calm me, even if he was doing it from the rooftop of another building. "How are we doing on our little friends?" I asked.

"Already took out two guards on the roof. It seems they were waiting for a helicopter. You're clear."

"Always watching my back, huh, Niko?"

"Of course I am. You do what you need to do."

Slowly, I worked on the lock mechanism. I tried to breathe and keep my hands steady. And then, finally, it let go, giving me a way into the room where I saw a bomb strapped to a chair. Jesus.

It was pretty standard. A detonator, charges, and a fuck-ton of C4.

If I got this wrong, the whole building was going to come down. There might not be anyone in this building, but there were certainly people in surrounding buildings, even though they'd been told to evacuate. I could see them as I'd run up the stairs, going about their lives as if nothing was wrong.

I had to do this. And I had to do it right.

I took out the rest of my tools. Holding the penlight in my mouth, I found the decoy detonator. I knew once I cut it, I would only have three minutes. I took a deep breath, thinking of Breck downstairs fighting. Hopefully he was out of the building by now.

"All right, Niko, I'm at the decoy. Is it the red or green wire?"

"You know, this is like a movie. You ask me which one, I tell you which one. You cut the wrong one, and instead of getting a steady timer, you get a rapidly declining clock, and you have to run for it."

"Jesus Christ, Niko, help me."

"I wanna say red. But this guy's a sadistic fuck, so I don't know."

"All right great, I'm cutting the red then."

"You sure, Sparrow?"

I thought of the last time that someone had asked me that question, was I sure. Hell, I had no fucking idea. I knew from the manual it said cut the red one. So that's what I did. The countdown time held steady with no acceleration.

I kept looking for the other detonator as my time ticked away in rapid seconds. But I couldn't find one.

"Niko. There's no second detonator."

He cursed. "Get out of there, Sparrow."

"Niko. Second detonator. There are people in the surrounding buildings."

"Sparrow. I got nothing. Get out of there."

Fuck Truman Nix. I hated him. I hated him for what he'd done to his wife. I hated him for what he tried to do to my friends. I hated him for what he was doing to me.

"Wild, is Breck out? Wilder, tell me."

"Breck knows how to handle himself. Get out of the building."

"No. I'm going back for him."

Instead of heading to the roof and flying off in my jumpsuit, which would have saved my life, I turned around and headed back the way I'd come. I wasn't going to leave him down there.

There was no way I was going to jump and save myself. We had to save each other.

But as I ran down the stairs, screaming for him in my comm unit, I knew our window of escape was decreasing rapidly.

When I made it to the room that we'd been kept in, it was empty. No Breck, no Truman. Just two guards, unconscious on the floor. "Shit."

I checked the detonation time on my wrist. Thirty seconds and going fast.

Fuck. I wouldn't be able to save Breck. All I could do was pray to God he'd gotten out in time.

I went to one of the windows on the north side and gauged my downward trajectory, wishing I had more height. But I didn't. At least this would be an easy floating landing since the building buttressed up to the river. I grabbed one of the office chairs, hefted it up with all my strength, and smashed it into the window. The glass was reinforced, so while it shattered, it didn't fall apart. So, I grabbed the chair and swung again. With the window out, I looked down. I stripped off my outer clothes, tapped the function panel on my squirrel suit to expand the wings under the arms, and swallowed hard.

I was out of time and out of options. I had no other choice but to jump. And so I did.

Chapter 19
BRECK

And the world came crashing down.

THE BUILDING SHOOK beneath my feet, and I whipped around. *Oh, shit. Shit, shit, shit.*

Sparrow.

Over my shoulders, I carried Truman out. I could've left him for dead, but I hadn't. Now I considered dropping him and running back for her. Would I have enough time?

I should have left him inside the building that was now crumbling around me. But I knew what Sparrow wanted. She wanted him intact and whole. And I could do that. I could give that to her, but Christ. *Sparrow.*

My heart shattered into a million broken pieces as it hammered too hard, too fast, and I worried. Had she made it out? Was she safe?

Into my earpiece, I screamed, "Does anyone have eyes on Sparrow, damn it? Any eyes. Right the hell now."

No response. It was just Truman Nix and me. Fucking hell.

A piece of my heart was in the building. And instead, I had to make sure that this idiot was okay. I resented that. I hated him. And I wanted to leave him right there and go back for her.

The ground rocked again.

And this time, cracks formed in the ceiling above me as I hauled ass down the stairs.

Fuck. Fuck.

On my shoulders, Truman groaned. "You're girl-friend's dead. And you're going to have to deal with the fact that I killed her."

"I swear to God if you don't shut the fuck up, I will kill you myself. Never mind that I went above and beyond to save your ass. I will kill you."

"You had better let me die. Because the moment I'm free, I'm coming back for her. Now that I know how strong she is, I know she's the right woman for me. I don't want to hurt her; I want to *own* her."

Deliberately, when I jumped on the next step, I jostled him so that his rib hit my shoulder, and he howled in pain. The building shook again. I could hear crashing somewhere from upstairs and behind us. Fuck.

I offered up a silent prayer to the God that had taken my parents from me. *Sparrow, please be okay. Please, please, please, please, please be okay.*

Truman Nix continued to taunt me. "Do you think you can keep a woman like her interested? Keep her entertained? Keep her challenged? You don't know what it takes."

"You're the one who doesn't know Sparrow. She doesn't need to be controlled. She's perfect."

"If you say so."

I finally reached the exit, ran to the SUV, and shoved him in. He flopped and groaned, curling in on his side.

I reached into the front seat for the walkie talkie. "Who has eyes on Sparrow?"

There was muffled shouting, and then my brother's voice was on the line. "Breck. You're okay?"

"I'm fine. Where's Sparrow?"

"She was trying to defuse a bomb, and then it went off. The building is collapsing in chunks. You need to get out of there."

"I'm not leaving without her."

"Breck. *Breck.*"

I shoved the walkie in my back pocket and ran back into the building and headed up the stairs. Jesus Christ. My family had never really been one for prayer. Sure, we made our state-required appearances, but it wasn't like any of us worshiped really. Christmas, Easter, that sort of thing. The national holidays of course. But at that moment, I spoke to God, Buddha, Allah, anyone I thought would listen. Anyone I thought would hear my plea, my plight, my wish, my hope. I prayed.

I booked it up nineteen flights of flying debris, and I followed the map that I had on my phone to where she was supposed to have been defusing the bomb. But at the entrance of the hallway, there was nothing but crumbled debris from the original blast site.

The ground shook again.

Wilder yelled in my earpiece, "Breck, get the fuck out now. The building's unstable."

"No. She's in here somewhere. I need to find her."

In a solemn voice, my brother said, "I'm not getting anything on her monitor. No heartbeat, no nothing."

All the breath left me then. In one long wheeze and exhale, I fell to my knees.

"Breck, are you there? Answer me."

"What do you read?"

"I've got nothing to read. You need to come back. Get out of there."

Oh God, she was gone. And a few days ago, I had left her because I couldn't stand the thought of her being hurt. Maybe if I hadn't walked away, we could have done this together, made a better plan with a better outcome.

"Breck, come on. This is not what Sparrow would have wanted. At the very least, get out so you can put Nix away for her."

Wilder knew exactly what to say to me, exactly how to get me to comply, because it was true. If I couldn't get to her, I could at least make the man who has caused her death pay. The man who had hurt her, the one who'd forced her into this predicament knowing full well that she would dive headfirst into doing the right thing.

I couldn't leave her. "I'm not going."

"Breck, listen to me. Sparrow's a smart woman. If she was capable, she would transmit. Do not do this."

"I have to be sure."

I shoved aside some of the rubble, climbing over the rest to get to the door, and then I lay back and shoved the full weight of my foot against the door. When it gave way, the room was dark, smoky, charred. "Sparrow.

Sparrow, please, God. Just say something. Move something."

There was static in my ears. Static... *and groaning.*

I looked around. "Anyone else catching that?"

"One second. I might have eyes." Wilder's voice in my ear was warbled.

And then it was Niko's voice. "I have a sighting. She made the jump. Breck, make the jump. She's on the ground."

The relief washed through me, making me nearly faint. "Jesus Christ. I'm on my way."

The problem was that once I was in, finding a way out was tricky. There was debris everywhere. But Sparrow had made it out. God, I hoped to Christ she was okay. At the far end of the room, I found the window she'd used. I searched below, but there was too much smoke to see clearly. She might have landed in the water. Had she made it out? I checked my comm unit as I stripped off my clothes and activated my suit, and then I jumped.

The air washed over my body as the ground rose up to meet me. I extended my arms and legs like I knew to do, then the glide happened. I might have even enjoyed the ride if I hadn't been so worried about Sparrow and trying to make my lungs fucking work properly. I'd inhaled too much smoke and soot. My lungs burned with every inhalation.

I glided to a landing at the opposite bank of the river, then I shed my suit and ran to the bridge to make it back across to the SUV. I stopped dead when I could see my way clear of the smoke.

Truman Nix. He'd been faking. He had his arm around Sparrow's neck, and she was struggling. She was so weak. "Nix, let her go," I commanded.

He shook his head. "No. I don't think I will. I think I'll keep this one. She's so spunky. Don't worry, I'm not going to kill her. But you will have to live with the knowledge that I took something from you. Just like she took something from me."

"Nix."

But he wasn't looking at me. He was looking down at Sparrow. She was whispering something to him. With Nix's attention diverted, I reached my hand to the small of my back where I'd stored the gun Nix had held on Sparrow earlier. How was my aim? Could I hit him? We'd all had hand-to-hand combat training. We'd all served in the military. Two years as was standard. I could do this. But, God, what if I hit her? He was leaning over her, and then I saw what she was doing. Even weak, with him choking her, she was still on mission. She reached into the little fold of her squirrel suit and pulled out the syringe. She said something that made Nix laugh.

I palmed my weapon even as she stabbed him in the chest. In that split second when he was screaming vitriol at her, I fired. Then they both slumped.

Chapter 20
SPARROW

One last chance at a beginning.

THEY SAY your life flashes before your eyes when you nearly die, but I thought that was a lie. I'd almost died a few times in my life, and I'd always been too focused how I could save my people and get out of the situation.

This time I only thought of one thing. One person.

Breck.

The sound of the gunshot echoed through my brain, and I blinked away the motion sickness, trying to catch up to reality.

"... Sparrow!"

I looked up, trying to see through the smoke and haze as I crawled from under the man on top of me.

My hand slid on blood, the sticky warmth coating my skin, and I cursed.

I was stronger than this. I could get out of this. I was fine.

I looked up, and Breck was running to me, his eyes wide, fear etched on his face in hard grooves.

"Breck," I coughed and spat out blood. I cursed under my breath, sucked in a deep lungful of air, and looked at the lifeless corpse beside me.

Truman Nix was dead. The man who had tried to kill my team, tried to kill *me*, was dead.

And I didn't know how Breck was going to handle knowing he had done it.

I had to help him somehow. If he'd let me. I almost laughed, wondering why those thoughts were coming to me at this moment. I shouldn't be worrying about that. I needed to get to my team, but my comms were staticky, and I couldn't say much. I just looked up at the man that I loved and swore I would do everything in my power to thank God that he was still alive and I was still here to watch Nix be dragged away later.

Everything hurt, and I wanted to roll over and just pass out, but not now. I had things to do first.

"Hey there, prince," I muttered. I tried to get up, but

my wrist buckled and my shoulder slammed into the ground.

"Damn it, Feisty. Stop moving. I need to check your injuries."

"I'm fine. I can handle this." My voice was already stronger, and I forced myself to a sitting position. Breck was there, cupping my face and sliding his hands down my arms. I winced at the sensation, and I saw him flinch before I cursed again.

"I'm fine. We need to check to make sure he's really dead."

That seemed to pull Breck out of whatever he was doing, and he finally looked at the dead body next to me and blinked.

"I killed him," he whispered. I reached out, and this time it was me comforting him, checking for injuries.

"You saved my life. You probably saved many lives."

"That's your job," he muttered, and then he shook himself out of whatever he was thinking, but I knew it was still going to be there for a long time. There was no coming back from that, from taking a human life, and he was going to have to work through it.

And, God willing, I wanted to be there to help him.

Maybe I really was a glutton for punishment.

"He's dead," Breck said, looking down at the man. "He's not breathing."

"Okay, is the team coming? I can't seem to get my comms to work." I tapped my earpiece and winced at the shrieking sound.

"They're on their way. They kind of watched me come after you, and they're probably never going to forgive me for that."

I narrowed my eyes at him and looked at the soot on his face, the cuts on his hands, and I let out a soft growl.

"I don't know if I'm going to forgive you. What the hell? What are you doing here?"

Breck's eyes clouded. "You could have died."

"I was going to say that to you. Breck, you shouldn't have come here. You could have been killed."

"Right back at you."

"How? I don't understand. Why did you trade places?"

"Because I needed to. He was after my brother-in-law. He was after you."

"And we had it. You didn't need to put your life on the line. I can't believe the others let you do that."

He shrugged then winced. He must be in pain from something, and I was going to kick his ass once I figured out it was. "I'm fine. You don't look it, though. Come on. We need to get you to a medic."

"Niko and the others are on their way," I said and tapped his earpiece. "Isn't that what you just said?"

He nodded and leaned into my hand. "They are. They'll get to us."

"Okay. Since neither one of us is bleeding out right now, do you want to explain to me exactly why you decided to put your life on the line?"

"Because, as I said, it was my family in danger."

"No, you don't get to do that, especially when you told me that you didn't want to watch me die doing my job. And now you do this? You risk everything? Come on Breck, what were you thinking?"

"I was thinking the woman that I loved was out here, and there was something I could do to help her. I am never going to stand in your way again, Sparrow. That I can promise you, but if there is something I can do to protect you? Protect Kannon, London, the baby? You can be damn well sure I'm going to do it."

I shook my head and immediately regretted it as the world started to spin.

"Shit, you're hurt. We need to get you somewhere."

"We will, but first, talk to me."

"I thought you were dead," he gasped, his whole body shaking.

"I'm not," I whispered.

"But I thought you were. The whole place went up in flames, and nobody could get ahold of you. And they kept trying to get me to leave, saying that it would be unsafe for me to go find you, and yet what did that mean for you?"

"My team knows what to do. They would have found me."

"I need you to know I'm sorry."

My eyes widened, and I coughed.

It must have frightened him a bit, and he said, "Shit, okay, this isn't the time for that."

"I'm fine," I said. "I'm fine. Tell me."

"I'm sorry. I know what you do, and I knew it from the first moment I met you, and yet I acted like such an asshole. But the idea of seeing you hurt? Look at me; it's killing me."

"What do you think it means to me to watch you be hurt? You're just as cut up as me."

"I think we can both agree to disagree on that," he growled out.

"This time maybe, but Breck? This is my job. I'm always going to be in harm's way. And I won't stop, but I can be smart. Not all assignments end with bombs and guns. Sometimes it's just really boring moments of me standing and watching to make sure the asset is secure."

"And I'd really rather that always be the case," he grumbled.

I nearly snorted but knew it would probably hurt.

"Okay, I agree, but that's not how it happens. I'm

going to be in the line of fire. I'm going to be in danger. And if we're going to be together, you're going to have to deal with that."

I heard feet pounding on the planks near us, and I knew my team was coming. I sighed. There was a dead body right next to us, I was bleeding, and so was Breck, and here we were, fighting, or maybe not. There was something happening between us, a shift, and we needed to finish our conversation, even if it was a mistake.

"I thought you were dead," he whispered.

I reached out, brushing dirt and soot away from his face.

"I'm not." I paused. "But I might be hurt again in the future, and you being here? I don't know what it means, but it can't erase everything that happened."

"I know. I'm sorry. I'm so fucking sorry that I left. We should have talked it out. I'm sorry. I fucking love you so much, Sparrow. I shouldn't have walked away. I should've been able to deal with my fears. And I don't know why they're so irrational, considering my family has always been in the spotlight, and that has an element of danger to it too."

"That has something to do with it most likely," I said readily.

I heard Niko shouting and the others coming toward us, and I knew our time was short.

"I know you're sorry, and I love you too, but this is your second chance. There are no more after this." I let out a breath as his shoulders dropped. "I love you, but I don't deserve to be treated like that. I understand why you walked away, but this is me. If you don't accept who I am, then this isn't going to work."

Breck leaned forward and brushed the hair from my face. And then Niko was there with the rest of the team coming along behind him.

"Love you too," he whispered, and I knew Niko and everyone else had heard. They'd probably heard the entire conversation over the comms, but I didn't care. They already knew nearly everything about me as it was.

Breck pulled back a little and said, "I might growl at you because that's who I am. But I'm always going to be there for you."

"But never as a decoy," I snapped. "Never again."

Breck gave me that playboy smirk of his, and I nearly smacked it off his face. "I can't promise that."

Then he lowered his mouth to mine, gently brushed my bruised lips, and pulled away. "I can promise you almost anything, but I can't promise I won't care for you."

I looked at him as the authorities arrived, and I knew they'd have questions that needed answers.

And I knew I had fallen. For my prince, the pain in the ass that never went away, and the one person I loved above everything.

Chapter 21
BRECK

A cold dark day begins with a colder morning.

IT HAD BEEN three days since I had shot and killed a man—three days since I had thought that the love of my life was dead.

It had been a long three days.

We were up in the family dining area, the one part of the castle that was for every single member of the Waterford family, and completely off-limits to everyone else. There were staff members available if we needed them, but sometimes we even cooked for each other. Not well, mind you, but we tried. Tonight, however, we had a full catered meal, thanks to Roman. The King of

Alden wasn't happy with any of us. In fact, he looked ready to murder all of us. After we healed, that was.

But since he couldn't do anything other than glower at us at the moment, he did what he did best. He took care of us, made sure we were fed, and now we're all huddled around the dining room table, the family sitting there as if we didn't help rule a country every waking hour of our lives, and sometimes when we weren't awake as well.

"I cannot believe you didn't send for us to come back for all this," London said, shaking her head. She had her hand over her rounded belly, and I wanted to reach out and see if she was far enough into the pregnancy that the baby would kick. But I had a feeling if I went anywhere near her at that moment, Kannon would probably stab me with his dinner fork. He was overly protective, and I didn't blame him. His team had been under fire while he'd been gone, and he had been protecting his wife, the princess and my sister, the entire time. He was constantly on edge, and I knew he was grateful he had Sparrow to lean on.

But considering I could still see the bruises on her face, and the fact that she had lost some of her hair at the bottom when it was singed off by the fire as she'd jumped out the window, I wasn't quite sure I was happy that she was second in command.

No, that wasn't quite correct. I loved that she was so good at her job. She was one of the best in the business, and while I was never going to be okay with the fact that she was in danger, I was learning to deal with it. That was growth. I wasn't always good with growth, but I was getting better. *Marginally.*

"Well, I'm glad that you weren't here," Sparrow said, and I gave her a sharp look.

"Ouch," London said, though she laughed.

Kannon nodded. "See? That's why I like working with Sparrow. She gets it. I wouldn't want you anywhere near an explosion." Kannon glared at me then Sparrow. "Not that I liked any of my team being there either."

"We took care of it, though." Sparrow looked at me and squeezed my knee. "All of us."

Wilder tilted his head as he stared at me, and I knew he was searching my face for something. I had a feeling I knew exactly what it was. "You sure you're okay?" he asked, his voice low.

But not low enough that everyone else couldn't hear the question. Then they all stared at me, and I cleared my throat before reaching for my water glass. I took a long gulp, just letting them stare before I nodded. "I am. And I'd do it again." I looked at Sparrow, right into her eyes. "Without hesitation."

She smiled softly, cupped my face, and then kissed me hard on the mouth before leaning back.

London clapped her hands while Kannon let out a groan. "Really, Sparrow? Him?"

"I ask myself that question every day," Sparrow said, deadpan, and she was very lucky we were in front of all of my family or I would probably have tossed her over my lap and spanked her ass. She must have seen exactly what I was thinking from the look in her eye, and she raised a single, defined brow. "Try it, prince," she muttered.

"Oh, I do believe I will, Feisty."

"Okay, now, none of that," London said, waving her hands in front of us. "Seriously. No eye fucking at the dinner table."

"I second that comment," Roman muttered, but he wasn't looking at Sparrow and me. No, he was looking at the other couple at the table.

"Thirded," Wilder said, and I just shook my head and laughed.

"Now that Kannon and London are home," Roman began, looking between all of us. "I think it's time we set a few ground rules as to what is to become of this family."

I groaned while glaring at London. "I'm blaming you for this."

She held up her hands. "I have no idea what you're talking about."

"She lies," Wilder said, grinning into his drink.

"What exactly is happening here?" Sparrow asked, and Kannon shook his head.

"I have no idea."

"We now have two new family members," Roman began, and I widened my eyes.

"Um," I began, and Sparrow snorted.

"Don't worry. There's no need for you to get down on one knee."

I coughed again, while everyone else at the table, including Roman, began to laugh.

"Um, continue what you were saying," I said, gesturing toward Roman.

"Once you remove your foot from your mouth, I will explain," Roman said, his eyes twinkling. "With new family members, and yes, Sparrow, you're family. You already were because you're like a sister to Kannon, but now you've also managed to completely transform my brother."

"Thank you," Sparrow said, leaning back in her seat. I put my arm around the back of her chair and played with her hair. I couldn't stop touching her, and I needed to know that she was real. Alive. Safe.

We weren't going to be safe forever. There would

always be something putting her in danger, but I was going to have to learn to deal with it. After all, I'd learned how to face other things in my life. I could do this too.

Because I loved the way she fought, the way she faced the world, I loved that more than anything, so I wouldn't stand in her way ever again.

Nor would I stand in my own.

"As I was saying, maybe it's time for us to ensure we continue to keep our family secure."

I frowned. "What do you mean?"

"I mean, it has been a while since we've had a family dinner like this," Roman said, looking between all of us. "Maybe we should re-institute it. Weekly."

My brows raised. "We see each other nearly every day," I began, but Roman shook his head.

"We see each other in passing. While we're dealing with the council, or while London is working on her new career, or planning a nursery. Or when Wilder is working on a thousand different projects at once." He gave me a pointed look. "Or when you were building a tech conglomerate in secret."

I winced but didn't say anything. My secrets had come out in full force during the investigation, and there was no more hiding it from anyone else. I honestly wasn't completely sure why I had worked so hard to hide it before, other than I had wanted something for myself. And maybe that had been selfish, but I didn't think I would have gotten where I was without trying to prove myself without the family's support.

But now I needed to make sure that I didn't have any more secrets when it came to my family. I had almost lost Sparrow, and honestly, I almost lost my life right along with her. I knew time wasn't guaranteed, so maybe I needed to stop hiding from everybody.

"We can do that," London said. She looked between all of us, her face glowing. I didn't know if it was happiness, marriage, pregnancy, or all three. Probably a mixture of everything. "I want to make sure this little one gets to know his uncles... and aunts," she said pointedly at Sparrow, and I resisted the urge to roll my eyes. "I don't want this little one to ever feel that they don't have a huge, bustling family. So yes, I don't want to miss out on what's going on in the family, even if I'm not here. If I have to video call into dinner when we're traveling, then I will."

"Same here," Wilder said, and I nodded right along with Roman.

"Good, then it's settled. We will get to know our family members again, even our new ones," he said, looking between Sparrow and Kannon. The two just stared at each other, before shrugging.

"Well, then, this should be interesting," Sparrow said, smiling.

"Just a little," I muttered.

"Now, I realize, Breck, that you enjoy your job, and you're doing wonderful outside of the family," Roman began, and I looked up sharply.

"I am. Is there something you wanted to say?"

"I was going to wait till we were in private, but since we're family, we might as well get it out in the open."

I tensed.

"If there's anything that you want to upgrade within the estate, or anything that you want to do when it comes to royal business, just let me know. I'm never going to order you to do anything, Breck. I never have." He paused. "Not really."

I snorted. "That's true," I said, a little wary.

"But you should know, while I'm pissed off that you never told us what you were up to, I'm so proud of you. I always have been. You're not a fuck-up, despite what others think."

I felt Sparrow tense against me, but I just brushed my fingers along her shoulder, and she calmed.

"I wasn't talking about you, Miss Bridges."

"You can call me Sparrow. I am dating your brother."

"True. And you did save his life."

"He saved my life, too," she said fiercely.

"So I hear. Breck seems to be a man of many secrets. But Breck? Like I said, you were never a fuck-up. Ever. You are welcome to put that brain of yours to good use within the family, or keep up with your business. I get that you want something of your own. I get that all of you do."

And I knew Roman couldn't have that. He'd never know the joy of having something that belonged only to him because he was king. I might be the heir, but Roman was the one with the world on his shoulders. And though I didn't know when or if he would ever get married, not after everything that had happened to him in the past, I hoped one day he would have his heir. Then again, with the way things were going, maybe London's baby would be the next heir.

Unless of course, I had a little honey-brown skinned baby with gorgeous green eyes and dark hair that looked just like her mom. I guess I should think harder about that ring, more than the fact that I had already bought it. Because I loved Sparrow, I just figured we needed a few more months before I took that big step.

But with the way with everybody was looking at us, maybe not.

Roman cleared his throat. "With Kannon Security firmly established on the island, our kingdom will flourish. I know you're working outside of the country too, but you are helping keep Alden safe as well. Keeping our family safe. You're working directly with Wilder, who is doing much of the same."

"It's my job to keep you safe, big brother," Wilder muttered, and I had to wonder exactly what Wild did every day. Because some things he kept out in the open, but most he didn't. He was even more secretive than I was. And that was saying something.

"Either way, we're working together, for good of the country and the family, and maybe those two should be flipped in order of importance every once in a while," Roman said, not looking at us now, but at his wine glass.

"We know our duties," London whispered. "And you're one of our duties," she said fiercely.

Roman winked, though I didn't see much humor in it.

"Perhaps. However, now that this business with Truman Nix is done, the media will no longer be paying attention to it. After all, the man was corrupt, and it seems the whole world is glad that he can no longer hurt anybody else." There was a growl in his voice that I agreed with, and although the media had been hounding us for the past few days, the rules on Alden when it came to media were different than most countries, and it kept us safe.

"Now, let's finish our dinner, have dessert, and talk about the next issues that will arise with the council," Roman muttered.

"Should I be here for this?" Sparrow asked, glancing at me.

"Of course. You're already sworn in as part of security, and you're mine. You go where I go."

She snorted. "I do believe you have that backward."

I grinned, leaned down, and captured her lips in mine, ignoring the groan from Kannon and the others.

Sparrow was here in Alden and wouldn't be leaving except for assignments in other parts of Europe. I would have to let her go, and maybe sometimes she would let me go with her. But we would learn how to deal with all that. But first, before any of that, I would enjoy a night with my family, where they knew more about me than I'd ever let them see before. Where I finally felt comfortable, like I wasn't the screwed-up playboy who only wanted to get in a girl's skirt, but rather the man who was in love with a woman who was stronger and fiercer than anyone I knew.

And even though the worst had *almost* happened, it hadn't.

And I would always remember that, always remember the woman at my side. And one day soon, I would ask her to be my wife, my princess.

I couldn't help but grin.

"What are you thinking about?" she asked softly as the others spoke.

"Oh, nothing," I mumbled, kissing her again. She gave me a look that said that I would have to explain later, and I would.

Because I would always tell my princess protector what was on my mind, even if I knew she would growl at me later.

Chapter 22
SPARROW

Happy ever afters can even surprise the prince.

"I CANNOT BELIEVE you got me into a dress," I said as I scowled. I tugged on the bunch of fabric near my hips and tried to lower it a bit so I wouldn't show so much leg, but there was no helping it. The red silk fit to my skin perfectly, as if it had been tailor-made for me. Of course, it had, and I knew it cost more than anything else I'd ever purchased in my life. However, it had been a present from Breck, and I was going to have to learn how to deal with it.

Even if I might throw up later just thinking about it.

"Well, I can't wait to get you out of that dress," he

purred, before he kissed me softly beside my mouth. "I don't want to mess up your lipstick, so I will save those lips for later. I can't wait until they're wrapped around my cock. Just imagine those red lips licking up and down my shaft as I slowly fuck that sweet mouth of yours."

I pressed my thighs together and glared at him, barely managing not to topple over the wineglass in my hand. "Stop it, Breck Waterford. What the hell are you doing? Somebody could overhear."

"We are tucked away in the corner while everybody stares at us two lovebirds wondering exactly how you could be so idiotic as to fall for little old me."

I rolled my eyes and downed half of my drink. "I'm pretty sure they're not thinking that. More like *Wow, he really went for a commoner this time, didn't he? Just like his little sister,*" I muttered, annoyed with myself.

Breck frowned and then rubbed his thumb along my cheekbone. "Hey, enough of that."

"Sorry, I'm fine. Really. I'm happy. So fricking happy. It's a little scary how happy I am."

"That's what I like to hear." He rolled his eyes and kissed the other side of my mouth. "Okay, now we're at a royal event where I am His Royal Highness Prince Breck, and you are my guest."

"Yes, Price Breck and guest."

"And my love, my Sparrow, my princess protector."

I narrowed my eyes at him. "You cannot call me that. I'm not a princess."

I swallowed hard as he gave me a look that told me that wouldn't be the case for long. He was going to propose one day, get down on one knee and do it just right, exactly how Breck would, because that's the kind of guy he was. And I was going to say yes. Because I couldn't resist him. I loved him, and I wanted to be his wife.

His princess? Not so much. I could handle the protector part, but the princess part was going to take getting used to. Including the whole dress thing all the time.

"You look amazing in that dress, and while I am going to fuck you hard in it, first, I want to dance with you in it."

I shook my head and set my drink on the tray of a passing waiter. Breck did the same with his glass and then took my hand. "Come now, let me show you exactly how I can move."

I rolled my eyes. "Oh, I know exactly how you move, Prince Breck."

"I love when you call me that. You get all sarcastic. It makes me hot."

"I'm pretty sure a stiff wind can make you hot."

"Well, you got the stiff part right, but only for you" he mumbled as he took me in his arms and twirled me around the dance floor. Others muttered as they looked at us, and I knew they were wondering how this could happen. Had I truly tamed the beast? Not so much. There was nothing tame about my playboy prince. However, I wasn't very tame, either. I glared at a few women who were ogling my man's ass, and though I agreed with them that he had a fine ass, it was mine. They weren't allowed to ogle like they wanted to touch it, and might just do so.

"Hey, stop scaring everybody."

"They look like they want to see you naked." I paused. "Possibly again."

He rolled his eyes and gave a quick glance around the room. "I can positively say I've only slept with one person in this room." He gave the room a second glance. "Yes, only one person. And that would be you, just in case you were having trouble with the math."

"I would kick you, but then I would trip in these heels. And then I would have to deal with the fact that I'd be on my face on the dance floor, and everybody would laugh at me. And I'm not in the mood to deal with that."

"I would never let you fall," he whispered, before he kissed the side of my mouth again.

"You always say the sweetest things. Sometimes the dirtiest things, but I like those too."

"Good. Now, is that a knife on your thigh, or are you just happy to see me?" he muttered.

I raised a brow as he spun me around. "It's a knife. I'd have my gun too, but it was too hard to conceal in this dress. So thank you for not allowing me to be fully armed."

He groaned and spun me again. "Damn, I don't know why that's so sexy."

"Because you have a weird kink I didn't know about?" I asked, and laughed.

"Possibly. But how weird. I thought I knew all my kinks. I'm so glad that you're helping me find them."

"Please, no more." I shivered, thinking about exactly what we had done the night before. "Let's wait on more kinks."

We twirled so that my back was to the wall with no one behind me, and he slowly slid his hand over my backside and gently patted me on the ass. "Sore?"

I groaned. "No. Now please, you're very lucky I love you, because if I didn't, I would be very upset thinking people know exactly what we did last night."

"They don't; they only wish they did." He spun me out to the middle of the floor, where Roman danced with London and Wilder danced with someone I didn't recognize. She was a young woman, but I saw a wedding ring on her finger and assumed she was married.

"Who's that?" I asked.

"The wife of one of the council members."

"And who's glaring at them from the side."

"Ah, that's another story," Breck muttered before spinning me again.

"You're making me dizzy."

"You always make me dizzy, Feisty."

"Wow, I stepped right into that line, didn't I?" I asked.

"You really did. Having fun?"

I looked at the laughing people, the glittering lights, and the man in my arms, and I smiled. "Surprisingly, yes."

"Well, that's good to know. And tomorrow, you can take me to the gun range, and that can be our date."

"Like I said, weird kink."

He grinned. "Maybe. And the night after that, we can sit alone in our bedroom, and we can watch movies or read a book or do nothing. Because it's not all this, Sparrow. I might be the heir to the throne, but I can treasure moments of peace as well."

My gaze traveled over to Roman as he brought London back to Kannon.

"But not everyone in your family gets that option, do they?" I asked softly.

His gaze followed mine. "No. At least not yet. But maybe one day."

There was another story there, but I knew he would tell me eventually. I was learning them slowly. Learning everything about him. I had never expected that this would be my life. That I would be dancing in a ballroom with a prince and happier than I had ever felt.

"This is only the beginning," he whispered.

I looked up at him then. "Really?" I asked.

"I promise. Just you wait and see."

And as the dance turned to a slower one, I leaned my head on his shoulder. And as we swayed, I let him lead. I wouldn't normally let anyone else do so, but this was Breck, and I was allowed to soften just the barest of moments.

I hadn't meant to fall for the man I had thought my enemy, the heir to the throne, but I had.

And now I was going all in, full force, with my heart wide open, my soul in his hands, and my future in the stars.

And I wouldn't have it any other way.

DANGER
SPARROW

"WHAT IN THE world are you doing?"

Breck kept trying to unzip my corset as he nipped at the back of my neck. "I'm trying to help you get undressed."

"We are at a party. A party for your sister. And my boss."

"I know. But I'm trying to help you."

I turned in his embrace and looped my arms around his neck. "How is this helping? You're trying to undress me in public. We have a party to attend. Welcome home for London and Kannon. Welcome the impending baby. Lots of guests. There are a hundred people in this ballroom."

"I know. But I'm helping you."

"How is this helping?"

"You look itchy."

Well, he wasn't wrong. I was itchy. London had brought me something that she and Rian had cooked up in Paris. The thing had a corset. And tulle. There wasn't a piece of cotton in sight. Not one piece. God, it was itchy.

And I couldn't really move that easily in it.

"You are incorrigible. Why don't you dance with me?"

"How about we dance here?"

"In the shadows? Where you can fondle me in peace?"

He grinned down at me and kissed the tip of my nose. "Now you understand. Trust me, everyone expects me to disappear from these things."

"Yes, I remember."

He winced. "But no one expects you to. So this way, everyone will think we're still here somewhere. Look, you've reformed me already."

"You recognize that you don't need reformation, right?"

His gaze softened as he watched me. "If you say so. I just, I love you."

"I know. I love you too. You think I'd wear this for just anyone?"

"I'm honored. Thank you. It does amazing things for

your tits." His gaze lingered as his voice went low and raspy.

I rolled my eyes even as a giggle escaped. "Breck. You cannot say *tits* in a ballroom."

"Why not? I like *tits*. *Tits* are my favorite thing on the planet. God, your *tits,* in particular, are spectacular."

I giggled. "You're the worst."

"Yes, but you love me."

"Yes, I do. Even if you keep saying tits."

"And you know what?" he asked. He leaned close to the shell of my ear. "Your tits are my favorite tits."

I couldn't help it; I gave him a snorting giggle. And he tickled me. Actually tickled me. The squealing was unavoidable.

Wilder walked by us and halted, apparently surprised to still find us present. "I'm surprised you two are still here. I figured Breck would have dragged you out by your hair by now."

"Oh, so he told you his plans?" I said as laughed.

Wilder shook his head. "Nope. I just know my little brother."

Breck had the decency to look sheepish. "No. I'm letting her enjoy the party."

London waddled over, with Kannon close behind. "There you are. Rian and I were trying to get a picture with you in this dress."

I groaned. "I wear dresses sometimes."

Kannon raised a brow. "Name one. Just one time."

"The Oscar party that one time. I wore a dress."

He shook his head. "No, you wore some kind of wide-leg pant thing with pockets. It only *looked* like a dress."

I frowned. "Semantics. Also, mind your business."

His smile was warm. "Well, you look lovely."

London took my hand. "Come on. You can't deny a pregnant woman."

"Oh, God. You know you can only use that pregnancy for so much longer."

She shrugged. "I'm baking a human. I can make that excuse for however long I want."

I shrugged. "Good point."

As London wrapped her arm around me, I could see the love in Breck's eyes as his gaze followed me.

Wilder nudged his shoulder and said something to him that made Breck blush. What in the world? I'd have to ask him about that later. I couldn't help but smile. This was my new family. I never thought I'd ever be this happy.

"Thank you, Sparrow."

I squeezed London back. "For what?"

"For mending my brother's broken heart."

"I'm not sure his heart was ever broken."

"Oh, I don't know about that. Breck's held himself apart for a very long time. And to see him with you, just open and laughing and so in love it hurts. I know that's on you. So, thank you."

"Well, I think I've got the better end of this deal. He's kind and loving and... God, look at him."

London rolled her eyes. "Do I need to remind you that I'm pregnant? I have a very limited gag reflex."

I laughed. In a corner, Roman and Rian were arguing about something. The king looked irritated, but also... I don't know. He was staring at her intently, his scowl evident. Rian had her hands on her hips, and she looked like she was giving no shits about something, which seemed accurate for how Rian dealt with Roman. The two of them were constantly bickering. And for good reason. Roman had been a complete dick to her the first few times they met. And Rian was having none of it.

London looped an arm through Rian's, and she jumped. Roman looked irritated that we'd interrupted them. I smiled up at him. "Your Highness."

He gave me a sharp nod. "Oh, why don't you two take Rian away. She's irritated me long enough."

I was shocked that he would even say that. And London looked pissed. But Rian just laughed. "Please,

I've been the most entertainment you've had all evening. You're sad to see me go."

Roman glowered at her. But Rian, in her red, deep V-cut couture glory just turned her back on him and sauntered away with us.

"Your brother's such a pain in the ass. You know that, London?"

London laughed. "Yes. But he seems to be more of a pain in the ass with you."

"God, he's such a rude asshole."

London frowned. "Did he say something he shouldn't have?"

"He certainly was up to something that he shouldn't have been. Kept digging himself deeper into a hole, calling me some kind of debutante. Then, of course, I had to remind him that he's the one who's royalty and a despot."

London winced. "Oh boy, you two never quit. Aren't you a match made in Hell?"

Rian huffed, "It's not me. I am perfectly pleasant to be around. He's the problem."

"I know, he's a pain in the ass. But just try and have fun, okay? For my sake. I think I'm about to pop, and I can't play referee."

Rian sighed. "No referee required."

We managed to find a photographer, and the three of us huddled together, Rian and I with a hand each on London's belly. Little baby Adams kicked hard, and London groaned. "God, she is kicking up a storm. Usually on my bladder."

"Oh God, that sounds terrible."

London got a dreamy look on her face though. "It is terrible. And also awesome. Oh! I have to pee. I'll see you guys later."

As she waddled off with Kannon's gaze tracking her, Rian gave me a tight hug. "You look happy, Sparrow."

I lifted my gaze to seek out Breck.

"I am happy."

At that moment, Breck's gaze lifted and held mine. And then he gave me the devil's own grin. And I knew that later, he'd be peeling this dress off me with his teeth. And I would absolutely enjoy it.

"I'm extremely happy."

My phone buzzed, and I glanced down at the message. Onyx texting, 911.

"Hey, Rian, give me a second. I just need to make a call."

"Sure. I'll just go grab more of that delectably expensive champagne."

"All right, thanks."

I marched out into the hall and dialed Onyx immediately. "Hey, what's up?"

Her sob was harsh. "Sparrow, I wouldn't call if I could avoid it, but I need help."

The hairs on the back of my neck stood at attention. "Where are you?"

"I'll text you the address. Can you come get me?"

I froze. "You're here?!" What had gone wrong that she had come to Alden?

"Yes, I'm in Alden. I had nowhere else to go."

"You stay there. I will come for you. But stay safe. Stay hidden. Don't move. You hear me?"

"I understand."

Before I hung up, she called my name. "Sparrow?"

"Yeah, Onyx?"

"Thank you."

I wasted no time marching into the ballroom to find my future husband and my future brother-in-law.

Breck noted my mood right away. "What's the matter, Feisty?"

"I've got a problem." I turned to Wilder. "And I'm going to need both of your help."

For more information please go to Carrie Ann Ryan and Nana Malone's websites.

WANT TO READ A SPECIAL BONUS EPILOGUE FEATURING BRECK & SPARROW? CLICK HERE!

A Note from Carrie Ann & Nana

Thank you so much for reading **ENEMY HEIR!!**

The Tattered Royals Series:

Book 1: Royal Line

Book 2: Enemy Heir

WANT TO READ A SPECIAL BONUS EPILOGUE FEATURING BRECK & SPARROW? CLICK HERE!

Acknowledgments

Nana and I would love to thank so many people for helping us get Royal Line completed!

Thank you to our editors, Angie and Laura, for helping Sparrow and Breck find their way through our twisted minds.

Thank you to our amazing cover artist, Jaycee for somehow figuring out what we wanted without even asking. Thank you to Wander for this fantastic image!

Thank you to our friends and teams for being there for us while we were having far too much fun in royal times and forgetting the real world if only for a moment.

And thank you dear readers for being so fantastic! Here is to more royals!

~Carrie Ann & Nana

About the Author

Carrie Ann Ryan and Nana Malone have been writing romances for over a decade. Between them, they have over two hundred romances under their belt to date!

That means they love romance, happy ever afters, and growly heroes, and the idea that love is love is love is love.

They were fangirls first, then friends, and now writing partners. Their Tattered Royals series is just the start...and they can't wait to see what comes next.

Find out more at each of their websites:

www.CarrieAnnRyan.com

https://nanamaloneromance.net/

Also from Carrie Ann & Nana Malone

With nearly two hundred heart pounding and thrilling romances between them, they figured they'd show you the best place to start with both of their works!

Loved Royal Line? This is where to go next:

From Carrie Ann & Nana:

The Tattered Royals Series:

Book 1: Royal Line

Book 2: Enemy Heir

Start here if you'd like to read Carrie Ann Ryan:

The Montgomery Ink: Boulder Series:

Book 1: Wrapped in Ink

Book 2: Sated in Ink

Book 3: Embraced in Ink

Book 4: Seduced in Ink

Book 4.5: Captured in Ink

Start here if you'd like to read Nana Malone:

The See No Evil Trilogy:

Book 1: Big Ben

Book 2: The Benefactor

Book 3: For Her Benefit

CPSIA information can be obtained
at www.ICGtesting.com
Printed in the USA
BVHW091139151121
621687BV00013B/734